WIND SPIRITS

By Jack Fetty

WIND SPIRITS

"Jesse, Jesse Brookes, get in here." I had been sweeping the front porch of the general store when Mr. Sol Siegel, the owner yelled at me. He insisted on keeping the little entry way free of dust and dirt so it wouldn't track into the store and now he is in a big toot to have me help him in the main store room.

As soon as I entered the store the short round bespectacled middle aged Mr. Siegel rushed up to me. He whispered, "Jesse you have to watch those sticky fingered Morrison twins. They always have their dirty hands in the candy jars on the front counter."

I don't know why Mr. Siegel worried about losing some penny candies to the Morrison twins. After all if he thought they had stolen some candy he would take that amount out of my meager wages at the end of the month.

I walked up to the front counter where the two jars of candy sat. I thought I would do the smart thing and just take them off of the counter and put them on a high shelf behind the cash box. That ought to fix those two. Usually one of them would cause a commotion of some kind to distract me and the other one would dip into the candy jar. Not this time.

My parents died three years ago and I have been working here every since. As much as I don't like working here I don't want those dirty little urchins to make me pay for their stolen hard candy.

When the one little snot nosed dirty faced brat came up to the counter and didn't see the candy jars he stuck his tongue out at me. I took a kick at him. He was too quick for me. I missed him. It is a good

3

thing his mother didn't see me. She would have yelled at me and defended her thieving little urchins to Mr. Siegel. He would probably fire me.

I wouldn't care if he did. I am seventeen years old and could get a better job than this one. My pay was a small amount of money each month and a place to sleep in the back store room. The store room also served as Mr. Siegel's office. He had a small desk and a dirty crumbled box which served as a place to file his papers.

Mrs. Morrison finally took her unruly children and left the store and I went back to sweeping the porch off. I don't think that she bought anything. She was probably just there to give her brats a chance to steal candy.

I finished my outdoor job just as it was getting evening time. The shadows were lengthening and the air was cooling off from the early spring sunshine when I saw a rider approaching from the west. By squinting against the setting sun I could make out who the rider was. I was surprised to see that it was my uncle Frank. Uncle Frank was my dad's brother.

I was surprised to see him riding up for tomorrow was Sunday and I always went to Frank's farm house for Sunday dinner.

Sunday dinners were their way of trying to keep me in touch with family. When my parents died Frank and his wife took myself and my two younger sisters in. They had four daughters and with my two younger sisters and me it didn't take long to figure out that it was too crowded in the house.

Since I was the only male it made sleeping arrangements rather awkward so I left to work and stay here at Mr. Siegel's store. I understood and I didn't have any ill feelings toward them about the arrangement, besides my little sisters had a great home to be brought up in.

"Hi Jesse, are you about ready to quit for the night? Or is that old tight wad going to make you work all night?" Uncle Frank smiled as he spoke. He said it good naturedly. He smiled a lot and rarely showed any displeasure.

"No, I am done working. All I have left to do is to tend to Mr. Siegel's mare that he keeps out back in the corral. What is going on? How come you came to town this evening?"

Uncle Frank dismounted and strode up the porch steps two at a time. He was a tall muscular good looking man with a well-trimmed full mustache on his upper lip. There are some people that say that I favor him in looks, of course without the mustache.

"Instead of coming to our house for dinner I would like you to meet me over at Shawn O'Toole's farm. We could spend a day working to spade up Mrs. O'Toole's garden and put the potatoes and some other garden crops in for her. Spading up the soil and working it into a fine enough seed bed for a garden is too hard a work for a thin young women with two young toddlers."

"If you meet me there early in the morning we can get a lot of spring work done for her. I'll have my wife make us something for dinner and I'll bring it along. Can you be there and help me out?"

"Yea, sure I can do that. I know the way. I'll ask Mr. Siegel if I can ride his white mare. He won't refuse if I explain why I am going to O'Toole's farm. Are you going to sit a spell before you head back to your place?"

"No, I'll have a drink of water and head on back. The wife will have supper ready for me. I can't keep her and that houseful of girls waiting."

"Uncle Frank, doesn't Mrs. O'Toole have a husband?"

"Don't you remember him? You have seen him. He is a little taller than I am with broad shoulders and a lot of dark black kind of wavy hair."

"He ran out on his wife. Mrs. O'Toole told my wife that when they got married that her daddy gave them some land and livestock to get them started in farming. Shawn O'Toole never liked farming and after a couple of years he up and left. Said he would find something better to do and when he did he would write his wife or come back and get her. It never happened. I think it has been going on close to two years now."

That night after work Mr. Siegel was most agreeable when I ask to use the mare to go help Mrs. O'Toole put in her garden. The next morning I had the mare saddled and was gone by the first real good light. It would take only an hour or so to get to her place and I wasn't in any hurry to start the back breaking job of using a spade to turn up the sod and then using a hoe and hand rake to make it smooth enough to plant a garden in.

On Sundays Uncle Frank's wife always fixed a great meal and I got to see my two little sisters. Eating a cold sandwich and working my butt off spading up a garden for some old farmer's wife isn't my idea of a way to spend a nice spring Sunday. At least I had enough sense to find an old pair of leather gloves and a wide brimmed hat to protect me from the hot sun while I was busting my rear end working in a garden.

Charitable Work

Sunday morning I rode up to the O'Toole place and didn't see any one. I figured that the garden was probably around back. After I hitched the mare up at the front of the house I walked around back where I saw Uncle Frank spading up the sod in the garden spot. No one else was around. That figures, the old gal got someone else to do the work and disappeared.

Uncle Frank was in the garden area and he had been working long enough that he had broken out in a sweat. He stopped long enough to use the forearm of his shirt to wipe away the sweat from his face. "Come on over here. I have another spade. The two of us can get this sod turned over in a short time."

He was smiling as he spoke. Just like Uncle Frank, sweating and working hard for someone else and yet always in a good mood. There wasn't a fence around the garden spot. That made me wonder if the raccoons and rabbits were going to get more to eat than Mrs. O'Toole.

"Morning, Uncle Frank, have you been here long?" I asked as I drove the blade of my spade into the stubborn sod with the weight of my body pushing down on my foot that was on the spade.

"Just a short while, had to visit a minute or two with the Mrs. before I got started."

"Where is the lady of the house?" I smirked, my question wasn't in a pleasant tone.

I was startled by a voice. "I am right behind you." The voice I heard was pleasant and rather musical and very feminine, not at all hoarse sounding like I expected it to be from a farm wife.

I had been caught saying something that was rude. I stopped working and turned around. I am sure my face was flushed with embarrassment and probably got even more flushed when I saw the farm wife for the first time.

Standing before me was a tall slender very attractive young woman. She had raven black hair and a lovely face. She was holding a toddler in her slender tanned arms.

She saw my discomfort and spoke softly. "My youngest was not having a good morning. With me, my children always come first. I had to go inside to comfort her, so I apologize for not being here to greet you."

I was embarrassed as I stammered out my apology. "Sorry, if I sounded out of line." Not knowing what else to say or do, I turned and started digging.

She didn't leave but offered an introduction in a soft but firm voice of a person that had been taught to be well mannered. "I am Rebecca O'Toole and who might you be?"

I stopped spading but was unable to look at the young woman as I mumbled a reply, "I am Jesse Brookes, a nephew of Frank Brookes. I hope your youngens get to feeling better." To avoid any further embarrassment I went back to work.

She didn't respond to that but I did hear the swish of her long skirt as she turned and went back into the house.

After she had left, Uncle Frank couldn't miss the chance to poke fun at me. "That went well, didn't it?" He about busted a gut laughing out loud at my discomfort.

"Darn it, you could have told me about the Mrs. O'Toole." I stammered.

Uncle Frank answered with a rather annoyed tone "What did you want me to tell you? That Mrs. O'Toole was nice looking and about your age or maybe two or three years older than you. Now let's get to work."

Within the hour Mrs. O'Toole brought a bucket of fresh water and a dipper out and set it in the shade of an oak tree that was nearby. Nothing was said and we continued to work spading up the sod of the garden area.

By noon we had the spading done and had started using hoes to chop at the turned over sod to break it up fine enough to rake down into a seed bed. We stopped work and sat in the shade of the oak tree. The sun had warmed the air up enough that we were both sweating pretty heavily. The slight breeze and the shade cooled us down, but I still felt like removing my shirt while we ate the sandwiches that Uncle Frank had brought.

We had just finished when Mrs. O'Toole came outside with a small basket. She came over to us and leaned over and gave Uncle Frank two huge pieces of chocolate cake. "Here, I hope you men enjoy this. I apologize that I didn't have any ingredients around the house to make some frosting."

In preparation to taking my shirt off I had unbuttoned it. With my open shirt I jumped to my feet and stammered, "Thank you, Mrs. O'Toole. I am sure that the cake will taste just fine without frosting."

"We don't have to be so formal. Why don't you call me Rebecca and I'll address you as Jesse." With that she smiled. Her whole face lit up when she smiled and her eyes seemed to have a deep warmth to them. That was the first time that I noticed what color her eyes were. They were a light green. Her eyes were unlike any color of eyes that I had ever seen.

She had a very pretty face, with little creases at the corners of her mouth when she smiled. I was so dumb struck with how pretty she was I didn't respond until she had turned and taken a few steps back toward the house. As she walked away I offered a lame, "Thanks for the cake, Rebecca."

It was mid-afternoon when we finished getting the soil smooth enough for planting. Uncle Frank said, "You rest awhile, I'll go fetch the Mrs. and ask her where in the garden that she wants each row planted. It might be better if you put your shirt back on before the Mrs. comes out."

I walked over to the oak tree where the bucket of water was and used the dipper to pour cool water over my sweaty head and chest before I put my shirt on. Uncle Frank and Mrs. O'Toole came out the back door just as I was struggling to get my shirt over my wet back.

I saw Mrs. O'Toole look my way as I pulled my shirt on. She smiled at my discomfort as I struggled to cover up my naked chest. I got my shirt on but to save myself further embarrassment I didn't attempt to tuck it inside of my pants. I stood rooted to the ground in the shade while the other two scratched in the soil to mark where each row of vegetables would be.

I waited for Mrs. O'Toole to start walking back toward the house before I went down to join Uncle Frank.

Uncle Frank informed me, "I have a Jersey milk cow that acts like she is going to give birth very soon. So I'll stay until we get the seed potatoes in the ground. I want to get home before sundown so I can check on that cow."

Uncle Frank smiled and said with a laugh, "Do you think that you can keep from stuttering and getting a red face long enough to have the Mrs. help you put the smaller seeds into the ground?"

"Darn it, the both of you caught me by surprise. If you have to leave I am grown up enough to know how to act."

Soon after that conversation Uncle Frank caught up his horse and waved a good bye to me just as Mrs. O'Toole came out of the house. This time she had both of her little ones with her. She was carrying the youngest and the other one, a little boy, tagged along at an

9

uncertain walk partially hidden behind his mother's skirts. He was eyeing me and measuring me to see if I was going to be a threat to him.

She took the children over to the oak tree and sat the little one on the ground and produced some carved wooden toys and rattles and such for them to amuse themselves while she helped me plant the small seeds.

"Jesse, we have already marked where we want the rows. None of these little seeds need to be very deep. I will show you how deep to make a little furrow and I'll put the seeds in the ground the proper depth and distance apart. Then all we have to do is cover them with a light covering of soil. I'll water them tomorrow. How does that sound to you?"

"Ma'am, I haven't done much gardening, so you are the boss."

She admonished me, "Jesse, remember, my name is Rebecca."

We finished just as the sun was beginning to set in the west and the two little children were entertaining themselves crawling around in the grass when Rebecca gently touched my bare forearm and looked up at me with those beautiful green eyes. "Jesse, I have a pile of wood that needs to be split small enough for my cook stove. Do you think that you could come back next Sunday and split that for me? If you come early I can cook us a nice dinner."

Rebecca was still touching my arm when she stopped talking. She then slowly ran her fingers down toward my hand before removing her fingers from my arm. As she did so she moistened her lips and smiled. "Why don't you come early in the morning before the sun gets too hot?"

I was sort of surprised at her touching me in that personal manner. After hesitating for a few moments I answered. "Rebecca, I would be glad to do that for you."

I was riding back home toward Mr. Siegel's store when my thoughts kept returning to Rebecca. She wasn't much older than I and such a nice looking lady. Then I would scold myself, and remind myself that she is married and has two little children. I shouldn't be

10

thinking about married women in any way but how I can help her by doing a man's work for her.

Before I knew it I was back at the store. The ride didn't seem to take very long. I felt very happy. When I was opening the gate to the horse corral I begin to whistle a little tune.

I was unsaddling the white mare when I noticed how long the shadows had grown. It would be dark soon. I was in a very good mood and hummed and spoke softly to her as I rubbed her down.

Mr. Siegel had gone home. He left the back door unlocked so I could get into my little sleeping area inside of the store room. I felt so good that I didn't go inside until it had gotten dark and the moon was beginning to appear in the east.

The next week went by slowly and at times I couldn't help but think of Rebecca. I tried hard to not think of her but she kept creeping into my mind. Finally, it was Saturday night. I was locking the front door of the store when I remembered that I hadn't asked Mr. Siegel if I could ride the mare tomorrow. It would be a rare day if he came to the store on a Sunday. I will leave him a note in case he comes back and misses the mare.

Sunday morning, I woke up later than I wanted to. The sun was up and I could tell by the still air that it was going to be a hot day. It is too early in the springtime for this kind of heat. I didn't want the mare to get too hot so I kept her at a walk all the way to the O'Toole farm. It seemed to take forever to get there.

I was quite a distance from the house when Rebecca came out of the front door and stood on the steps and waved to me. It made my heart skip a beat to think that she must have been watching for me.

I dismounted and was tying the horse to the hitching rail when she gave me a cheery "Hello Jesse, it was getting late. I was afraid that you weren't coming."

I just stood there a few moments trying to think of something to say. I couldn't take my eyes off of her. She had the youngest child in her arms. Apparently the baby wasn't weaned yet for she kept trying to get inside of Rebecca's blouse. In the process the baby had

11

reached up and had messed up her mother's hair and left wet spots on the front of her mother's blouse.

Rebecca had on a freshly washed blouse that buttoned down the front. The blouse seemed a little small and her milk filled breasts strained at the fabric stretching it tightly over her breasts. Her skirt was long and came to her ankles. I was embarrassed that I was looking at her body and quickly looked down at the ground in front of me for fear that Rebecca had seen me looking at her in such a manner.

All I could think of to say was, "It is going to be a hot one today."

Rebecca recognized my discomfort and responded with a musical laugh. "I'll go back inside and feed this one. The wood pile and splitting axe is out back. See you in a few minutes."

I felt relieved that she had gone inside and went out back where I saw a large pile of fire wood. The pieces of wood were too large to be used in a kitchen cook stove and needed to be split. It was going to be a hot job and would probably take the better part of the day.

It didn't take long before I had worked up a good sweat. I rolled up my shirt sleeves and unlaced the neck of my shirt when I heard the back door open. I hoped it was Rebecca and that she was bringing me some cool water.

Rebecca came with a Mason jar full of cool water. She had left the children inside. She had smoothed out her blouse but there was still a wet spot over one breast that gave evidence that the baby had been busy taking nourishment.

"Here, Jesse, this will cool you down. It is fresh form the well, should be nice and cool." She looked at me with those pretty green eyes and a little half smile on her lips like there was something that was tickling her.

"Don't work too fast. You don't have to split all of that wood pile today." She laughed again. "You can leave some of it for seed."

I didn't understand that it was a joke and that she didn't really think that it would go to seed. "Thanks for the drink. I'll pace myself. I doubt that I can split all of this big pile of wood today. I might have to come back some other time to finish it."

"That would be all right with me. I will have lunch ready. It is warm enough that maybe we could eat over there in the shade of the oak tree. Yes, a picnic, would that be all right with you?"

It was well past noon and my stomach had been growling with hunger for some time when Rebecca came out of the house with our lunch. I was beginning to think that she had forgotten about her promise to feed me.

She went directly to the oak tree and spread a little table cloth out and placed several food items on it. Just as she was completing her task she looked up. "Come on and join me. I hope that you are hungry. I have put the children down for their nap, so we won't be bothered during lunch."

Because I was hot and sweaty I had my shirt open. It was much cooler in the shade of that big old oak tree and I began to fasten my shirt.

Rebecca smiled and said, "It's all right if you don't fasten your shirt up. I am not embarrassed or offended; after all I have seen bare chested men before. You have been working hard, so if you are cooler that way, I don't mind.

I sat down cross legged while Rebecca sat down in front of me. She was not directly in front but off a little bit to my right and facing me. She had stretched out her long legs so that they were beside me. The picnic lunch was directly in front of me and to her left. It made it easy for both of us to reach and get what we wanted to eat and we were close enough to one another to talk. I liked this position as I was close enough to Rebecca that I could almost touch her and I could see the sparkle in her green eyes.

We had finished eating when Rebecca leaned forward by propping herself up on her right arm her face was close to me. "Jesse, do you have a girl friend?"

I was slightly embarrassed and taken by surprise with that question. "Ahh, well no, I don't. Fact I never have had a girlfriend. Never had time what with me working six days a week and going to Uncle Franks on Sunday."

13

Rebecca leaned forward to within a few inches of my face. She licked her lips with the tip of her tongue. Her eyes were so pretty and bright, as if there were little lighted candles behind each one of them. "I guess that you have never been kissed by a girl then."

Before I could answer Rebecca had reached out and with her right hand behind my neck and head. She pulled me close to her and kissed me gently on the lips. With her face very close to mine she sighed and started to speak but then quickly changed her mind.

Her nostrils were flared and she was breathing heavily when she again licked her lips and put both arms around me and pulled herself up to kiss me more passionately. She kissed me again; this time with both hands pulling my face to her. Her lips were parted slightly as she kissed me with a great deal of passion. She held the kiss a long time and I couldn't help but kiss her back.

Soon I was holding her tightly in my arms. Rebecca pushed herself forward so that her body was pressed tightly against mine.

After a while she pulled away from me and with her eyes sparkling and her breath coming in little quick gasps she flashed a smile, "You're a fast learner."

After another passionate kiss Rebecca lay down. "It is very hot even under this oak tree."

Rebecca then unbuttoned her blouse exposing her full breasts. She stretched her long legs out wide and pulled her skirt up above her knees.

"You can lean down here and kiss me. Start with my lips." Rebecca arched her back and thrust her bare firm breasts forward. She repeated "Start with my lips but you can kiss me any where that you want to."

Startled by her brashness, I kissed her softly on the lips. I had pulled back to take note of her reaction when I noticed that both breasts were exposed. There was a droplet of milk that had oozed from within one of her breasts. It clung stubbornly to her nipple.

Rebecca leaned back a little further and unbuttoned her blouse further. She willingly exposed both of her milk filled breasts... "Kiss

me, I want you to kiss me. You can kiss me where ever you wish."
She said as she arched her back, pushing her torso toward me.

Rebecca knew what I was looking at. With fierceness she
grabbed me and pulled my face down to her breast. "Go on she
muttered kiss me there, take me in your lips, take me now." She
demanded in a low husky voice.

I showed no resistance, and with great joy did as she had
commanded.

My lips were moist and sticky when I felt Rebecca's long
fingers unfastening the front of my pants. After she did that I didn't
need anymore encouragement. I stood up and removed my britches
while Rebecca hoisted her skirt up to her waist.

We kissed and caressed and touched one another. We coupled.
When we were through we were both half naked lying side by side,
breathing heavily and not saying a word.

All at once Rebecca sprang to her feet. She was putting her
clothes back in order as she hurried toward the house.

I thought she had bolted toward the house because I had done
something wrong. Then I heard the feint sound of one of the children
crying. I realized that being a mother came first.

I was surprised at how late in the day it was. I went to the front
door and peeked in. Rebecca was nursing the youngest child. "I best
be going now."

Rebecca looked up at the sound of my voice. "The baby will
be done in a couple more minutes. Why don't you come inside and
wait before you leave?"

I was a bit embarrassed, but I entered anyway and sat down at
the kitchen table. With a soft sweet voice Rebecca said, "Jesse, I hope
that you will be back next Sunday. I do have more chores for you to
do. She hesitated, plus I want to see you." She finished her sentence
with a small come hither look and a radiant smile.

It made my heart miss a beat and I caught my breath as my
emotions soared. "I'll be here in the morning, ain't nothing can keep
me away."

The next thing that I remember I was in the saddle and was half way home. All I could think of was those bare arms and legs and that beautiful face so close to mine. *Rebecca, Rebecca, what a lovely sounding name.*

The next week crept by. I think it took for ever for Sunday morning to come. I was up early and had the mare saddled shortly after sun up. This time I remembered to ask Mr. Siegel if I could take the mare for a ride.

On the ride to see Rebecca I noticed how beautiful the spring flowers were and that the morning sky was so blue without a cloud in it.

Again Rebecca must have been watching for me for she came out of the front door just as I rode up. She quickly came down the three steps and took a hold of my hand and held it too her cheek. "Good morning, I wasn't sure that you would come." She said as she brushed her lips gently over my fingers.

I lost track of what went on for the rest of the morning. I know that I did some work, but I kept looking toward the house to get another glimpse of Rebecca. I wanted to hold her and kiss her, but was not sure if I should be so bold.

That question was answered when Rebecca stepped outside to talk to me. "After I put the children down for their afternoon nap I will come out with our lunch. We can have it under the oak tree just like we did last week."

We had lunch under the tree. We couldn't hold back our passion for one another. We did every thing that we had done in the past week and more.

I was about to leave and I wanted to kiss Rebecca good bye. But I couldn't get close to her because both of her children were awake and hanging onto her skirt and demanding her attention. Rebecca suggested, "Why don't you come late Saturday night next week? You can stay with me that night and we can spend all day Sunday together."

I don't remember how I answered. I don't even remember the ride back to the store. The next week drug by slowly. I could not get

Rebecca out of my thoughts. I couldn't wait until I would see her again on Saturday night.

Sometimes during the week I could see her face, those beautiful green eyes, that smile with the little creases at the corners of her lips. That is when I would feel uneasiness in the pit of my stomach. It was a good feeling.

I had been seeing Rebecca every Saturday night and all day Sunday for over two months now. She would share her bed with me and we would couple and make love through out the night on every week end.

Today was the ninth time that I had ridden the white mare up to Rebecca's front door. This time she didn't come out to greet me. She was so devoted to her children that I figure one of the children needed her attention.

"Rebecca" I called out before entering.

"Yes, come on in."

Rebecca was sitting at the kitchen table. The children were crawling around on the floor playing. "The coffee is still hot. Pour yourself a cup and have a seat."

I knew something was wrong. She always met me at the door or outside and would at
least give me a hug and usually a very warm friendly kiss. After I sat down I took a good look at Rebecca. She appeared pale and her hair hadn't been brushed. That was very unlike her. She always kept her hair brushed.

"What's wrong, Rebecca?"

"I was sick at the stomach and threw up again this morning. I have been sick every morning for almost a week now."

I was alarmed that she had been sick, "Do you want me to take you to the doctor? Or maybe I can get some medicine for you."

She shook her head and answered in a tired voice, "No, I don't need any medicine. I also missed my monthly." Rebecca sighed and looked at the floor as she ran her long fingers through her dark hair in an effort to make it lay down.

I said nothing; I didn't understand what she was trying to tell me. I felt helpless. I didn't know what was expected of me.

Annoyed, Rebecca scolded. "Damn, Jesse, don't you understand what I am telling you. I am with child. I am going to have another baby."

Once that news soaked in I was so excited that when I jumped to my feet I knocked the chair over. I went quickly to Rebecca and knelt beside her. I clasp her hand in mine. "That is my seed. It is our baby! Maybe it will be a boy."

She withdrew her hand and sat there with a long look on her beautiful face.

"Rebecca, what is the matter? Don't you want to have our baby? You seem real upset about this."

"Oh, Jesse, yes I am upset. I don't mind having more children. I love them and want to have more babies. It is just too soon. I would have liked to have waited for another year or two before I had another child."

That Saturday night was not like the previous ones. After they had put the children down Rebecca went directly to bed. As I pulled back the covers to get into the bed with her she rolled over and turned her back to me...

I lay there on my back with eyes open looking into the darkened room. I could hear the light breathing of the children and sometimes the sound of a cricket calling out for a mate by rubbing its legs together. I did not have any idea how to talk to Rebecca about her carrying my child.

"*Darn, I didn't even tell her that I loved her. I have never said that, maybe it would make her feel better if I did tell her that I loved her.*

The next morning as Jesse is getting up Rebecca ran outside. Jesse can hear her gagging as she vomits. She reenters the house and is pale and unsteady.

Rebecca's voice is weak and strained, "I think I would like to be alone today. Why don't you come back next Saturday night? I will probably feel better by then. It will give me some time to think everything over and set my mind straight about this."

"That is fine. Is there any chores that you want me to do before I leave?"

Rebecca said nothing and just answered with a weak shake of her head.

"I'll just be going now. See you next week."

Jesse saddles the white mare and as he is riding away he turns and looks back toward Rebecca's house in hopes that she would at least have come outside and waved at him or something as he left.

There wasn't any sign of her. Confused and disappointed about her reaction to being with child he kicks the mare into a gallop.

I can't understand why she isn't as full of joy as I am about having a baby with me as the father. Maybe it is mainly because she is sick. She will be more loving and back to her old self when she gets over the morning sickness. I don't expect us to couple like we have been, but she could be more loving toward me.

Jesse begins to think of spending the rest of his life with Rebecca as his wife. *We could live there on that little farm and fill that house full of youngsters. Uncle Frank could help me with the farming until I learn how. I have never thought of being a farmer until now, but with Rebecca beside me I could learn. Oh, I wish I had told her how much that I love her. Rebecca, Rebecca, how much I love you. I can't wait until next week so I can get down on one knee and ask you to marry me.*

It had been only two days since Jesse was at the O'Toole house. Mr. Siegel ordered Jesse outside to sweep the steps and the little front porch of the store. He was such a stickler on keeping that area clean and free of dust and mud. Jesses was half-heartedly sweeping as he day dreamed about more pleasant things. It was a warm late spring day with a soft southern breeze. Jesse was in no hurry to go back inside and stock shelves.

He looked up from his task to see a man walking slowly toward the store from the west. Jesse stopped sweeping and stood leaning on the handle of the straw broom, trying to make out the features of the man as he approached. The man was tall and had a full dark beard and long unkempt unruly dark hair. The dust from walking the dirt roads had settled on to and clung to his beard and clothes. The man looked vaguely familiar. He had gotten to within fifty yards of the store front when Jesse recognized him.

He almost choked as he muttered, "Oh my God, It is Shawn O'Toole!!!"

Shocked, Jesse dropped the broom and retreats to the safety of the store, hoping that Shawn will keep going and not come into the store. He cautiously looks out of the front window of the store and is relieved to see Shawn continue walking toward his home without so much as a glance toward the store.

At the O'Toole farm Shawn walked in through the front door. He came in the open door without knocking and surprised Rebecca. She sat down at the table in total shock. "Shawn, what a surprise. I thought you were dead."

"It has been almost two years since you left home and I haven't heard from you."

Her face was as white as a ghost with the shock of seeing her husband who she thought was dead.

"Don't I at least get a hug; after all I am back from the dead." Rebecca stands up and goes to Shawn. With no show of emotion she wraps her long arms around his waist and gives him a sisterly like hug.

It is very early in the morning on the third day since Shawn had walked in on Rebecca. The sun hasn't come up yet when the barking of several dogs awakened the O'Tooles. Shawn clad only in his long johns grabs his flintlock pistol and ran outside to see what is causing all of the commotion.

A small pack of stray dogs are barking at the horses. They have spooked the horses enough that the horses brake through the flimsy wooden corral fence and out into the open.

Once the horses realize that they have room to run they take off with the pack of dogs nipping at their heels.

"Damn it, those dogs won't stop chasing them until those horses are in the next county. It will take me two or three days to chase them down and get them home."

Shawn had run a few steps in his bare feet but stopped when he realized it would be useless to try and catch any of the horses until they quiet down. He turned back toward the house just in time to see Rebecca bent over and vomiting beside the back of the house.

Shawn entered the front door just as the pale disheveled Rebecca entered the back door.

"You threw up yesterday morning too." Shawn hurled the words at her in an angry tone. He sat down at the table. "I been gone for close to two years and when I came home all you did is give me a hug and a light kiss or two.

It wasn't any different when we went to bed. You used to be the one that wanted to couple all the time. It used to be that you couldn't get enough. Now when we go to bed you turn your back to me and go to sleep."

"You don't have any interest in coupling and you're sick at the stomach in the mornings." His voice got louder and angrier. The veins on his tanned neck stand out as he shouts, "Damn it women, I ain't no dummy, I can tell when your with child."

Shawn jumped to his feet and in one big step quickly closed the distance between them. He grabbed Rebecca by her hair and twisted. He jerked her head around and kept twisting until she went down on her knees to try to escape the pain.

She cried out in pain and pleaded, "Stop it, stop it, Shawn your hurting me."

"I'll hurt you a hell of a lot more if you don't tell me who's the father of that bastard child that's inside of you."

He pulled her to her feet by her hair and drew back a big fist to strike her.

Rebecca held up her hands and covered her belly with them. She yelled at him, "Stop if you make me lose this child I'll never speak nor see you again."

Glaring at her with face contorted and fists clenched Shawn let go of her.

He had released her so quickly that she almost lost her balance. To gain a little safety from his fists she sat down in the kitchen chair and scooted up close to the table.

With tears streaming down her cheeks Rebecca begged, "Shawn I have always loved you." She pleaded. "You know that, I loved you ever since I was a young kid of 12 or 13 years old. Shawn you're the only one that I have ever loved. But if you cause me to lose this baby it will be over between us. I'll take the other children and go back and live with my folks."

She saw that she was gaining the advantage in their quarrel. Rebecca explained in a steady and controlled voice, "You know that I love my babies more than anything else. It don't make any difference if my babies are alive and on this earth or unborn they are mine to nourish and to protect. When that seed comes into my body it is mine. I'll do what ever it takes to do that."

Rebecca's threat kept Shawn from striking her but his anger had not lessened any. His red eyes bulged from the sockets. He spat saliva as he spoke, "Who the hell is the father? Who have you been cozying up to in bed with since I been gone? I may not hit you in the stomach but I sure as the hell can put knots on your head unless you tell me that."

His eyes bulged and his rugged face was contorted so that he looked like an angry snarling animal.

Rebecca pleaded, "Shawn, you had been gone for almost two years. You never wrote, there wasn't any word from you. I thought you were dead."

With trembling lips and tears in her eyes she lied. "It was just once. I was already in bed and he got in bed with me. I couldn't stop him. I swear, Shawn it was only once."

Shawn was all too willing to lay the blame on the man for he truly loved Rebecca even thou in his eyes she had been unfaithful. The spittle flew from his open mouth and the veins stood out on his temples, "Just tell me the truth. Who is it?" he yelled.

On the other side of the room both of the children had been frightened and began to cry.

Rebecca thought, *I have to protect myself and my children, Jesse will just have to take care of his self. Besides, maybe I can get Shawn to quiet down and everything will eventually be all right.*

"Jesse Brooke, he works down at the store."   .

"Brooke, that must be Frank Brooke's kin."

Knowing the name of the father seemed to enrage Shawn even more. At least he now had someone that he could punish even thou his two year absence contributed to his wives infidelity.

He cursed and unable to strike out at Rebecca he kicked at his pack that lay in the corner of the kitchen. When he did his toe struck the neck of a full bottle of whiskey.

Shawn stared at the bottle as if he didn't recognize what it was. He then stooped down and picked up the bottle. He clamped his teeth down on the cork stopper and twisted the bottle with one hand until the cork popped out. He spat the cork stopper out onto the floor and took a huge drink of whiskey. He pulled the bottle from his mouth and with his eyes watering he coughed and choked as the raw whiskey burned his throat.

 This didn't help his disposition. Shawn angrily pulled on his pants and boots. With his unbuttoned shirt flapping about him he grasp the open whiskey bottle by the neck and plunged out of the door with the bottle in one hand and his flint lock pistol in the other hand.

 He cursed some more as he realized that his horses were gone and he was a foot. He began the long walk toward the store and Jesse Brooke.

Shawn had been walking and drinking for sometime. The bottle was only half full. Drinking the whiskey on an empty stomach had quickly brought him to a state of drunkenness where he had lost his sense of reasoning.

Shawn had been carefully taking one step at a time and just as carefully keeping both eyes glued to the ground in front of him to avoid stumbling and falling down. He was startled when he almost walked into a horse and rider that was standing still directly in front of him.

Shawn stopped and in his drunken state slurred an inquiry, "Where the hell did you come from?"

"Shawn, I have been sitting here on this horse for several minutes waiting for you. I am surprised that you didn't see me."

Shawn waved the half full whiskey bottle at the rider. "So I am here, now get the hell out of my way. I got business to take care of. Who the hell are you anyway to hold me up?"

"Shawn, don't you recognize me? I'm Frank Brooke, your neighbor. You have been gone for a long time. What are you doing out here afoot?"

"It's good that you ask, cause I'm going to the store to teach your kin, Jesse, a lesson."

"What is going on, I don't understand. What did Jesse do to get you so riled up?"

Rebecca said, "That the son-of-a-bitch raped her and got her pregnant. I'm going to make him pay for that. Now get out of my way." Shawn dropped the whiskey bottle and fumbled to get at the pistol that he had jammed down into the waist band of his britches.

Frank was unarmed and quickly realized that the drunken Shawn might start shooting at him. With a jerk on the reins he abruptly turned his horse around and kicked her in the ribs. The startled animal leaped a head and was soon going full speed toward the store.

Frank was a quarter of a mile from the store when he began shouting Jesse's name. Jesse was inside the store by himself when he heard the commotion and ran outside just as Frank arrived. He jerked back on the bridal reins to bring his horse to a dusty skidding halt in front of the store.

Bewildered Jesse asks, "Uncle Frank, what's going on? What is the matter?"

He could tell there must be a big problem. Frank never rode his horses that hard and the usually smiling uncle had a serious look on his handsome face.

24

Frank didn't answer right away he was busy quieting his excited mount. The mare had felt and responded to the excitement and urgency that her rider had. It took a few minutes for her to settle down and quit prancing around and breathing hard. Jesse understood this and waited until Frank was ready to answer.

"I saw Shawn O'Toole walking this way. He was pretty drunk and armed. He is coming here to do you some harm." Frank hesitated, in a low voice he continued, "He says that you forced his wife." He couldn't bring himself to use the word, rape. "And now Rebecca is with child. She said you are the father of her unborn child."

"Shawn is coming after you, Jesse. He may try and kill you. He is too drunk to think straight. You better come stay at my place until he cools down."

All Jesse could think of was Rebecca lying about him forcing her. Jesse questioned, "Why would she lie? I love her, she cared for me too. Uncle Frank, you know I wouldn't do that to any woman. Uncle Frank I love her. Why would she lie about us? It's been going on between us for a couple of months. I was thinking about marrying her"

Tears came to his eyes as Jesse pleaded, "You got to believe me, Uncle Frank. Why would she lie?" He repeated.

There were several minutes of silence before Frank spoke. He reasoned, "Often men beat their wives to take out their anger on them. Shawn has always had a bad temper. He might have threatened her and she lied to protect herself and the unborn baby."

Then in a quiet and reassuring voice Frank spoke again. "You better come home with me. O'Toole will sober up and in time this will blow over."

Jesse cast a wistful look toward the O'Toole farm, "No, there isn't any reason for me to stay around here. I'll just leave."

Bewildered Frank asks, "Where will you go? What are you going to do, walk? Come on home with me." He was becoming impatient with his young nephew's stubbornness.

"I'll take Mr. Siegel's white mare. I'll leave him a note and tell him that I will pay him some day for her. Maybe you can soothe his ruffled feathers on that account. He is such a stingy old man."

"Where will I go? I don't know the road heads west. I guess that is as good a direction as any. If I go to your place Shawn might follow me there. I don't want to put your family in any danger."

Frank argued, "That ain't sensible. You just come on with me."

"It's no use. I can't stay here. I don't want to stay in this country and be reminded of the past. Again Jesse looked forlornly toward the O'Toole farm. "I made up my mind. Mr. Siegel is sick and staid at home today. I'll take what I need and leave him an I owe you note and hope that he doesn't send the law after me."

"That is the way it is going to be, Uncle Frank. Now I got to get busy packing some things together and ride out of here. You tell all those women at your house good bye for me. Give my sisters a big good bye hug for me."

Jesse turned his back on Frank, straightened his shoulders and went back into the store. Frank knew that there was no use in arguing. He could do nothing but ride home and tell his family that Jesse was leaving.

Jesse entered the store and locked the front door behind him. He hurried into the office and bedroom and took some money out of a coffee can that he had hidden under the bed. He counted the money; it was $4.32. He opened the desk drawer and took out a sheet of paper. In the bottom of the drawer was an old partially rusted Belgium made 5 shot revolver. He picked up the revolver, looks at it and then stuffed it into the front of his trousers and put the box of cartridges into his front pocket.

Jesse spoke out loud as if he were talking to someone in the room. "Mr. Siegel won't need this. I have never shot a pistol before. It can't be too hard to do. When I went rabbit hunting with Uncle Frank he said I was the best shot with a rifle that he had ever seen, especially for someone so young. It will just be one more item that I owe Mr. Siegel for."

Jesse than sat down at the desk and wrote Mr. Siegel a letter explaining what he had taken and that he intended to pay him for the horse and other items as soon as he got a job.

Jesse closed the back door behind him, locked it and put the key on the door frame above the door. He quickly saddled and bridled the white mare, tied his bedroll of two blankets onto the back of the saddle. The pistol, shells, money and other items went into the saddle bags.

Before mounting up he looked around and was satisfied that there was nothing else to do before leaving. He guided the mare around to the front of the store and stopped.

Once again he took a deep breath and looked to the north toward the O'Toole farm. In the distance he could see a man on foot moving slowly toward the store.

Jesse started the mare off at a walk, following the dirt road to the west. He wasn't sure where it led except it might end up in the Missouri River. He just wanted to put some distance between him and Putnam County.

Jesse had been riding for about one half hour and couldn't help himself. Again he looked toward the O'Toole farm. He imagined that he saw Rebecca's face in the clouds. There among the fleecy white clouds her dark hair was in stark contrast with the white clouds. Her eyes were brighter and greener than he had ever seen. Her soft lips parted in a smile and those little creases became evident at the corners of her mouth.

Realizing that it was his imagination Jesse looked away, shook his head and took in a big deep breath. "I have to get far away from here." He spoke to himself in a loud clear voice.

He kicked the mare into a slow gallop. He kept her at that pace for a very long time. They came to the top of a hill and he could see that a small creek crossed the road at the bottom of the hill. He slowed the mare to a walk while she was going down the steep grade. He didn't want her to run downhill too fast and come up lame or sore.

They stopped at the edge of the creek. In order to allow the mare to drink more easily Jesse took the bridle bit out of her mouth.

27

He joined the mare for a drink from the slow flowing mud bottomed creek.

Sitting down on the creek bank he became more relaxed after the drink and having put some distance between him and the angry Shawn O'Toole and the stingy, Mr. Siegel.

Jesse took off his hat and ran his hand through his hair. It gave him time to think. He decided he should travel at night just in case Mr. Siegel sends the sheriff after him or Shawn gets a horse and chases him.

The white mare was a good easy riding horse but she was so darn white. During the day even a half blind man could spot her from a mile away. In was now late afternoon so he was going to have to ride all night long and sleep tomorrow during the day. It was going to be a long time in the saddle. He cautioned himself to not push the mare too hard if he wanted her to last.

The sun was rising in the eastern sky when Jesse pulled the mare up to a halt. He saw a dense growth of trees and underbrush near another creek. That would make a good hiding place to bed down for these daylight hours he told himself.

He awoke with a start. Sitting upright Jesse parted the brush and looked around. Although it was an overcast day he calculated that it must be about noon. There were crows cawing in the upper branches of the trees. Maybe that is what woke him up.

He had put hobbles on the mare so she had not ventured off. Still suspicious he untangled himself from the blankets and emerged from the cover of the brush to walk to the top of the hill. Seeing no sign of anyone satisfied him that he was just a little jumpy about being followed.

Jesse retreated to the cover of the brush and trees to try and get more sleep before dark and another night of riding. Riding to where? He asks himself.

Jesse saddled the mare just as darkness was falling. The sky was overcast. There would not be any moon light to ride by tonight. During the night the clouds became darker and it was threatening to rain.

He thought he could see the feint glow of lights in the distance. He reined his horse to a stop. By squinting into the dark night he was barely able to see what appeared to be the lights of a farm house. A short distance from the house he found a very dense growth of large trees. Jesse reined in the white mare as he had decided to stop early with the threat of rain he wanted to find some good shelter. A huge cotton wood tree looked like a good place to camp under to try and stay dry during the coming daylight hours.

Jesse had put hobbles on the mare again and using the saddle for a pillow he soon was asleep.

He awoke with a start to find that it had begun to rain. He was still dry, at least for the moment. There was thunder and lightening in the distance and it was moving in his direction.

Jesse was startled by a loud voice, "Hello in the camp." The voice came from the direction of the farm house.

Jesse cautiously peered around the trunk of the tree to see a man sitting bare back on a work horse. He had on a rain slicker and had pulled his felt hat down low so the rain wouldn't run down the back of his neck.

The farmer held up both empty hands to show that he meant no harm. "You can stay here under that cottonwood if you like. But I would offer that those damn trees are like lightning rods. Look around you and see how many times their bark has been split by lightening."

"If you would like, you can come up and stay in my barn until this storm passes.

The barn ain't much but it would be a lot drier and saver than this big old tree."

Jesse was already beginning to get damp and the lighting was moving in closure at a fast pace. "I would be obliged. My name is Jesse and I am not armed." He held his coat tails out as he spoke.

As soon as Jesse had accepted the invitation the farmer turned the old plow horse and headed for cover. He turned and motioned with a wave of an arm for Jesse to follow.

Jesse arrived at the barn door behind the farmer just as the rain began to pour down. By now the thunder and lightning were directly overhead. Bright jagged bolts of lightning ripped through the heavy moisture laden air, followed by the explosive claps of thunder.

They had both dismounted in the dark barn and looking out the door the farmer spoke. "This will pass in a few minutes. As hard as it is raining you'd gotten your britches wet if you would have staid under that tree."

He turned and peered into the inner darkness of the barn. "Molly, are you here? I can't see in there."

A soft feminine voice answered, "Yes, paw. Did you get wet and who is that with you?"

There were two empty horse stalls in the little barn. The farmer put the work horse in one and motioned for Jesse to use the other one for his horse.

"This young man is Jesse. When it lets up a bit you and I will go up to the house. You can bring this traveler a hot cup of coffee and something to dry him off."

Jesse never did see the owner of the soft voice. He never looked in that direction although he wouldn't have been able to see her as the walls of the horse stall interfered with his line of vision. He turned his back to the direction from which her voice came from. He busied himself unsaddling the white mare and rubbing the wet horse down with hands full of straw.

Soon the worst of the down fall was over. It had been a hard rain and the farm yard had become a sea of ankle deep mud. Jesse had finished rubbing the mare down and his damp clothes had made him chilled. He began to shiver and wished the owner of the soft voice would hurry up and bring him something to dry off with.

To Jesse's surprise the farmer climbed aboard of the work horses back again. "I have to go help the neighbor with some chores. Molly will help you. Make yourself at home here in the barn."

"Thank you, sir. I'll be leaving as soon as I get dried off a bit and I am sure there won't be any more lightening."

Jesse was standing alone and looking out of the barn door toward the house when he was surprised to see the girl named, Molly, dashing out of the door of the house toward the barn. He didn't remember seeing her leaving the shelter of the barn to go to the house.

As she ran toward the barn she was carrying a container of some kind in her right hand. Her head and shoulders were covered with a blanket.

Her free hand was holding her long skirt high above her bare white knees to avoid having mud splashed on to the otherwise clean dress. The barefooted young girl skipped along trying to miss the large puddles of standing water. The girl could not avoid having small clods of mud splattered onto the white skin of her sturdy legs. Her lower legs had mud freckles on them.

She entered the barn breathing hard. Her ample breasts heaved noticeably with each deep breath that she took. Her blonde hair had gotten wet and clung to her forehead in ringlets.

Embarrassed, the young girl let go of her skirt so that it would drop down and cover her bare lower legs. Sheepishly she looked down at the floor of the barn as she spoke.

"Here this is some hot coffee. I didn't bring a cup but you can use the lid of the canister to drink from." The young blonde girl sat the canister onto the floor of the barn. She then removed two clean burlap sacks from underneath of the blanket that covered her shoulders and handed them to Jesse.

"You can use these to dry yourself off." She offered as she continued looking at the floor.

Jesse took the burlap sacks and started to dry his head and arms off. A second storm had moved in. It had begun to pour rain again and the thunder and lightning seemed directly overhead. The thunder rattled the loose boards on the side of the barn and the lightening lit up the inside of the barn as if there were dozens of lighted kerosene lanterns hanging on the rafters and support posts.

"Thanks a lot for your trouble. Sorry that you got your legs wet." Jesse handed the girl one of the sacks. "Here, dry yourself off."

"That lightening is pretty close and it is raining pretty hard now. You better stay down here until it lets up again. It is too

31

dangerous to go across the yard with that lightening popping so close by."

Just as he spoke a bolt of lightning lit up the sky and a loud clap of thunder rattled the old loose wall boards once again.

Molly jumped from being startled by the loud thunder. She jumped toward Jesse as if she needed reassurance that she would be all right.

Jesse reached out and patted her reassuringly on the shoulder. "Your name is Molly, isn't it? You'll be fine as long as you stay here in the barn with me. The lightning storm will pass."

Molly moved close enough to be touching Jesse and looked up at him with fear in her blue eyes. "I am afraid of storms, just like our farm dog. Only the dog crawls under the porch when there is lightning. I can't do that."

Shivering she pressed herself against Jesse's chest. Jesse wrapped his arms about Molly's shoulders and held her close. "I am here, like I said I'll take care of you."

"Your dad seemed in a big hurry to run off and help your neighbor. Won't your mother mind him being gone all day?"

"I don't have a mother. Molly hesitated a long time as if trying to find the right words. "She passed on about two years ago."

Jesse continued to hold Molly with both arms. "That is all the more reason that he should stay here."

There was another long silence, Molly nestled her head against Jesse's shoulder and in a barely audible voice, "I think daddy is a courting the older daughter of our neighbor. He probably won't be home till dark."

Jesse leaned back to put a little space between himself and Molly. He reached up and brushed some of Molly's blonde curls from her forehead. He spoke softly, "Why don't you stay down here with me for a while? Let's have some of that hot coffee. Do you mind drinking from the same lid as me?" He managed a smile.

The two sat down in a pile of sweet smelling hay and made themselves comfortable against an interior partition of the barn. The storm had let up. There was only a very light sprinkle coming down.

"It sounds like the hard rain is over. Daddy says we need a down pour once in a while. That it cleans the creeks and rivers up by flushing them out. He says that everything starts a fresh then."

Molly looked up at Jesse with her blue eyes searching his face. "What are you doing, riding out here by yourself?"

"I have been living and working in a store in Putnam County but am tired of working for nothing and getting nowhere. I just decided to pull up and move on. So I decided I would pull up stakes. I am heading west. I don't know where I will end up

"Oh, that sounds exciting. I am tired of staying on this lonely old farm. Dad is probably going to marry that skinny neighbor woman. I don't know what he sees in her. She is tall and skinny and has bad teeth. One of the front ones overlaps the other one. "

"It is lonely here on the farm. Jesse, take me with you" Pleaded Molly. She pressed her body close to his in an attempt to persuade him. As she spoke Molly's face was very close to Jesse's.

Jesse thought, *"This little farm girl is trying awfully hard to get me to do her will. She is pretty, but not like Rebecca. Rebecca is such a beautiful woman. Oh, I can't seem to get her flushed out of my mind. Maybe me mind has to be like this storm cleaned out the creek. Maybe I have to see if I can flush thoughts of her by having thoughts of someone else.*

I might as well start with the flushing, "Molly, can I kiss you?"

Molly answered his question by merely leaned forward to meet Jesse's lips with hers. Molly's lips were fuller than Rebecca's and she didn't part her lips when she kissed but her kiss was warm and pleasant.

Jesse's strong arms pulled Molly in closure to him so that their bodies seemed united. Their kisses became more and more passionate. Jesse laid Molly down in the soft sweet smelling hay and kissed her throat while he unlaced her blouse with one nimble fingered hand.

Molly didn't make any attempt at stopping him. When Jesse slid his hand inside of her blouse to caress her full white breasts she moved her shoulders in a manner to allow him access to her body. A soft moan escaped her lips.

After they had coupled Jesse lay beside Molly and held her soft hand to his lips and gently kissed her fingertips. "Molly, you were wonderful. Are you all right?"

Molly sighed, "Umm, yaa," She murmured as she snuggled next to Jesse's chest. Jesse untangled himself from Molly's arms and stood up. He pulled up his pants and said rather matter factly, "It's quit raining. I guess I'll be going."

Shocked, Molly abruptly sat up and brushed the hay from her blonde hair. She then fumbled at covering her exposed breasts and pulling down her skirt. As she smoothed out her skirt she choked out a question. "Are you leaving? Don't go without me. Take me with you."

"I don't know where I am going or if I can feed myself let alone another person. You're really very sweet, but I am riding alone." Jesse had the white mare saddled and in one easy movement he swung aboard.

"Good bye, Molly." He looked down at her. She had tears in her eyes and looked very heart broken and forlorn. She did not reply but her lower lip trembled as she turned away there was a bewildered look on Molly's innocent young face.

Jesse didn't want to do anything further to hurt the farm girl so he rode away without saying another word. After he had ridden a few yards from the barn he turned and looked back. Molly was still bare footed and standing in the mud outside of the faded barn holding her blouse together with both of her arms crossed over her breasts. She made no attempt to wave.

That was the last that Jesse had seen of the once innocent, Molly. *Rebecca, damn it, 1 started thinking of her again. 1 was going to compare Molly to you in my mind. Maybe the flushing out didn't work so well. Is this all there is to having a relationship with a women? Am 1 going to compare every female that 1 meet to Rebecca? Rebecca, Rebecca, how long will it take to forget your lovely green eyes and warm embraces? It is not going to be easy to forget her.*

Frustrated Jesse kicked the mare in the ribs. She responded by quickening her pace to a steady trot. Trotting in the mud was slow treacherous going for the mare. There was a constant sucking sound as she would pull a hoof from the sticky mud and a sodden plopping sound as she drove it back into the mud again.

After the mare had slipped in the mud for a second time Jesse pulled up on the reins and slowed the white mare down. *It is better to go slower and be safe. Besides it isn't this horse's fault that I am upset. It doesn't matter how fast or how slow I go it will take some time for me to quit thinking of Rebecca every time I see a woman.*

The rain storm had cooled the air and Jesse pulled his coat collar up and buttoned it at the neck to stay warmer. He had been accustomed to sleeping during the daylight hours. The lack of sleep had begun to catch up with him and he began to doze off.

Jesse awoke with a jolt as his head snapped back and his neck ached from the sudden movement. He grabbed a hold of the saddle horn for support. Blinking his blurry eyes he was unable to make out where he was. He rubbed his eyes with the back of his coat sleeve.

Finally his eyes came into focus. The mare had decided to stop. She had walked up too a hitching post in front of a small town general store. The mare turned her head and looked up at Jesse as if to say, "I am too tired to go any further." Then she turned back and lowered her head until her chin was almost touching the wet earth.

"Hey, old gal, I'm sorry. You went all last night and most of this day without a break. Here it is almost dark again and you haven't had any rest nor feed and water for a long time. I'll get off and see where we are and then I'll rectify your lack of rest and vittles."

Jesse rubbed the mare's neck and wrapped his arms around hers. "Good girl. I'm going into this store and see what this little town is called."

Stiff and sore from being in the saddle, Jesse painfully climbed the three steps that led into the store. He knew that it would have been better for him as well as the horse to have taken a break. He was sore and exhausted from riding for almost twenty four straight hours. His legs felt weak and rubbery, each step took a lot of effort.

The little store reminded him of Mr. Siegel's store. It had been only a couple of days but it seemed like ages ago that he had been working there.

A voice came from the back of the store, "Hello, what can I do for you?"

"Hello, I been riding all day and fell asleep while in the saddle. My horse brought me here. I wondered where I ended up."

"This is the town of Conception. Do you need to get any provisions?"

Shaking his head, Jesse responded, "No sir, I don't need anything. Am I still in the State of Missouri?"

"Yes, young man you are. If it would help any to get your where abouts, St. Joseph, Mo. is just a half days ride to the south."

"I thank you sir. I have never been this far west before. What will I find in this town called St. Joseph?"

"You can find about anything there. There is good things and bad things to be had in that city. And it is a city. Why I heard that they have three or four thousand people living there. Then there are the wagon trains that stop off there for provisions on their way west."

"Like I was saying there are a lot of good folks in that town, but you got to keep up your guard cause there are those that would take advantage of an inexperienced soul."

"St. Joe is a busy place, what with the number of people using it for a jumping off place to head from civilization into the wilderness that will take them west. I don't understand, they is a looking for glory land with nothing but milk and honey when they could stay right here in this country."

"The first obstacle that they encounter is the Missouri River, after these rains, it's going to be running pretty high. Then there are the Indians and a lot of rough country for the tenderfoot fools to cross." The store keeper shook his head. "I just don't understand."

"That horse looks plumb tuckered out. You better take care of her or she won't last the trip. I got a little bit of oats and some hay if you got fifty cents I could let you have them for that white horse."

Jesse reached in his front pocket and touched the solitary silver dollar that rested there. He didn't take it out of his pocket.

"I don't suppose there is any work I could do to pay for that feed?"

The store keep shook his head. "No, sorry, I am all caught up and ready to close for the day."

Jesse left the silver dollar in his pocket. "I guess I'll just have to walk her out of town and find a good patch of grass for her. Thanks for the directions and the advice."

He was in hopes that the owner would feel sorry for him and gives him the feed and a dry place to sleep for a while. Jesse turned and walked slowly to the white mare. He heard the door being shut and latched behind him.

Untying the mare he led her toward the outskirts of the tiny town. There wasn't more than four or five houses in the town so it wasn't long until he came upon a meadow where the grass was tall and there were some trees to bed down under.

Jesse took the bit out of the mare's mouth and hobbled her so she couldn't go far. He spread his tarp out on the cold rain soaked ground under a large red oak tree. He pulled the saddle blanket up to his chin and used the saddle for a pillow. It made a poor bed but it was the best he could do. Soon he was a sleep.

The tarp kept him dry but it didn't stop the cold from penetrating to his tired body. It was only a few short hours before Jesse awoke, cold and shivering he sat upright and hugged himself in a futile attempt at getting warm enough to lie down again and get back to sleep.

Disgusted with his inability to get any sleep he stood up, stomped his feet to get the circulation going and wrapped his blanket about his neck and shoulders. Jesse than looked around the meadow for the white mare.

There were some clouds hiding the full moon. Soon there was a break in the cloud cover. A mother raccoon was running across the clearing with five baby ones trailing after her. The babies tumbled over one another and ran here and there but always ended up trailing after their mother.

The white mare hadn't wandered far away. She was a sleep standing next to a deep pool of water that had been formed in a low area of the meadow by the recent down pour. Far above them in one of the trees an owl started hooting.

"Come on mare, if I can't sleep neither can you." Jesse saddled the startled mare and was soon on his way through the dark toward St. Joe, Missouri.

It wasn't quite daybreak when the bone tired Jesse and his equally tired horse came to the darkened outskirts of the small city. A solitary barking dog announced Jesse's arrival as he rode down the dark main street. Jesse couldn't read the signs on the buildings. He could merely see the shadowy outlines of buildings on each side of the street. With clouds obscuring the moon it was too dark to identify any of the businesses.

Arriving at the west end of the main street Jesse was able to identify the shape of a stable outlined against the dark sky. He dismounted and led the mare inside the pitch dark interior of the barn. Stumbling in the darkness he located an empty stall. Stepping inside of the stall he detected the sweet smell of hay in the manger. He led the mare inside and tied her reins to the metal ring attached to the manager.

Jesse rolled himself over into the manger. He had only enough room in the manger to sleep in a folded up position. Within minutes he was sound asleep.

"Hay, what the hell are you doing in my barn?"

The loud gravelly voice was enough to awaken Jesse with a start and scare the mare. The mare jerked her head up and started to retreat but was stopped by the reins that were tied
to a metal hitch ring that was attached to the manager for that purpose. Jesse sat up and peered toward the end of the stall where he saw a large man in bib overalls and ragged felt hat. The man had a pitch fork in his large callused hands.

"This ain't a free hotel. Now get the hell out here and pay me for your night's lodging."

Jesse offered an apology, "It was very late at night when I got here. No one was around and I wasn't about to wake you up at that time. Besides I didn't mean to stay with out paying." Jesse hoped that explanation was sufficient to keep the burly stable owner from using that pitch fork to enforce his rules.

"Fifty cents for the two of you. That will take care of you until dark tonight. You can feed the horse some hay. But no grain, mind you or that would be another fifty cents." The stable owner held out his dirty hand while impatiently waiting to get paid.

"Do you have any work for me to do to pay for my keep and the horses too?"

"What the hell, do I look like I can't do my own work? I want hard cash, now!!!"

He growled as he shifted the wooden handle of the pitchfork from one hand to the other with such force that it made a muffled smacking sound as it hit his hardened palm.

Jesse stepped out of the darkness of the horse stall to where the owner could see him. He threw his shoulders back and drew himself up to his full height. He didn't want the owner to bully him anymore and wanted to show that he was a full grown man.

Jesse stood a couple of feet in front of the owner and looked him directly in the eyes. "I will give you a silver dollar for the days stay and I want my fifty cents in change back now." He demanded with what he hoped sounded like he meant business.

The owner stepped back two paces and took a good look at the tall well-built youngster. After measuring Jesse he reached in his pocket and brought out a fifty cent piece in exchange for the silver dollar that Jesse had offered.

After the stable owner had left Jesse spoke out loud to no one in the empty stable. "Well that was a nice wake up call." He gathered up some fresh hay for the mare and found himself a quiet out of the way place where he could stretch out and lie down on a fresh pile of hay. He was asleep as soon as his head settled into the pile of hay.

It was mid-afternoon when Jesse had finally had enough sleep. He stood up, stretched and yawned and rubbed the sleep from his eyes with the back of his hand. He was just getting ready to clear his throat of phlegm when a voice from the other end of the barn interrupted him.

A man called out in gentle voice "Are you the overnight border?"

Jesse turned to face the owner of the soft gentle voice. He was surprised to see that the voice belonged to a tall slender muscular man in a faded blue work shirt and dirty patched work pants.

"Yes sir, I am. And who might be asking? I have paid my days keep to a man that said he was the owner."

"Was he a dirty big man that cussed a lot? If so that was the owner. I am Sam, the stable hand. If you are a stranger to St. Joe, maybe I can give you some directions. There are a lot of people passing through on their way west. They are looking for provisions and the like."

Jesse removed his hat to scratch his head. He then spat on his fingers and used them to smooth down his tangled light brown hair before putting his hat back on his head. He rubbed his flat belly in a circular motion. "I sure am hungry. I am so hungry I could eat a horse."

After taking a moment to think about what he had said Jesse smiled and chuckled. "I guess a horse stable isn't the best place to say that."

Sam smiled and walked to the front of the stable. He stood in the front door and pointed to a small building that was about 100 yards from the stable. "That is a café. The lady that cooks does a good job. She is clean, won't be any rotten meat or wormy mush and she is reasonable. You can get a decent meal for twenty or twenty five cents.'

"What with it being the spring of 1845 and the settlers coming through here on their way west prices are kind of high. Matter of fact, there was a small group of sod busters left here just a couple of days ago."

"Thanks, Sam; I'll try that little eating place."

Jesse crossed the street as he approached the café he detected the pleasant aroma of cooking wafting on the breeze and he inhaled deeply to experience the smells better.

There were only three small crudely built mismatched tables and chairs in the small café and all of them had customers sitting at them. One table had two men sitting at it. They hadn't been served yet. One of them glanced up at Jesse as he entered the room.

The man that looked at Jesse was a bearded fellow that appeared to be in his fourth decade of life. He looked like a laborer with dirty clothes and rough hands. None of the men had removed their hats. When the man saw Jesse looking for a place to sit he beckoned at him. "You can sit with us." He said as he pointed at an empty chair across from him at the little table.

Jesse nodded a greeting at the man and then remembered his manners and removed his hat. "Thank you for the invite. My name is Jesse." He offered as he sat down and stuffed his hat beneath the chair.

Both men looked Jesse over as if trying to find any clues as to whom or what he was. Neither man offered their name nor stuck out a hand to greet Jesse.

Leaning back in his chair Jesse offered to start a conversation. "I just rode into town last night. I'll be looking for work. Would either of you two gentlemen know where I might find a job?"

The bearded man that had waved him over to the table answered. "We drive freight wagons. I don't think our boss needs anyone else. We're just going thru town so don't know of any work that be had here in this place."

A stout middle aged woman delivered two large plates full of food and sat them down in front of the two men. The plates barely touched the table before the men had started cutting the meat and shoveling the meat, potatoes and stewed tomatoes into their mouths.

The woman looked at Jesse, and used her apron to wipe the perspiration from her red face. "Well what do you want to eat?" She demanded in a rough unfriendly voice.

Jesse looked at the large steaming stakes. The saliva filled his mouth and he inhaled deeply to savor the aroma of the cooked meat.

"All I have is fifty cents. Is that enough to get one of those?" He said as he pointed at one of the now half eaten steaks.

Without answering the women turned and hurried back into the kitchen.

The two men ate quickly and loudly smacked their lips and wiped their mouths and beards on their shirt sleeves when they had finished their food. After wiping their mouths off they leaned back in their chairs and with a satisfied look on their faces they burped loudly. Without saying a word to Jesse the friendliest one left a silver dollar on the table and they left.

After a short wait Jesse had his meal placed before him by the unfriendly sweating heavy set women. After eating the fine meal he fumbled in his front pocket and found the lone fifty cent piece and brought it forth. It seemed like an awful lot of money for one meal. He left the money on the table and walked out the front door.

There was a couple hours of daylight left as he stood on the board walk in front of the café. Jesse took a few moments to stand and look around the main street of St. Joe. The town was indeed a busy place as people were loading wagons with merchandize and hurrying from one destination to another.

Directly across the street was a saloon. The sound of a piano playing came through the open front doors. A rider had just reined his horse at the hitching post in front of the saloon and was preparing to dismount. There was something vaguely familiar about the rider. Squinting his eyes and with furrowed brow Jesse studied the man.

"Oh my Lord, it is the sheriff of Putnam County." After identifying the man, Jesse stepped back into the shadows of the café.

The sheriff secured the reins of his horse to the hitching post, glanced both ways down the street, hitched up his trousers and entered the saloon.

Jesse took a deep breath and stepped out of the shadows into the street. He walked at a steady unhurried pace down the street toward the stable. He felt much safer when he reached the shadowy door way of the stable out of sight of the saloon.

Jesse spoke with a whisper to himself. *"I wonder if Mr. Siegel turned me in to the sheriff as a horse thief. Maybe the sheriff is after someone else. I can't take that chance. But where will I go and what will I do?"*

"Did you have your supper at the café?" The voice came from within the stable.

Startled, Jesse jumped as if he were shot. He wheeled around to face the direction of the voice. "Sam, is that you?"

"Yea, who did you think it was, one of the horses?" Sam found his answer amusing and replied with a loud boisterous laughter.

"Oh my Lord, that is the second time in the last two minute that I have been surprised. Yes, the meal was very good. Sam, I don't think that I want to stay here this night. I heard that there was a wagon train that left here recently. Do you know how long ago that it left?"

"Maybe three days ago, are you expecting to catch it?" What is your hurry? You just got here. A strapping young man like you should be able to find work here in St. Joe."

"Let's just say that I got a bee in my bonnet and a hankering to see some country beyond the Missouri River. Will it be easy for me to pick up the trail of those wagons?"

"Boy, you sure the hell is in a lot of hurry to leave. You shouldn't have any trouble following them. As soon as you cross the river the ruts are pretty easy to see. It might take you a couple of days to overtake them. I don't know how charitable they would be taking on a stranger with no means of supporting yourself."

"Thanks Sam, I have made up my mind. I'm riding out of here just as soon as I can saddle up. Would you go to the café and get me some vittles to take with me? Here is my last two dollars. Get me whatever you think I might need."

Jesse forced the money into Sam's callused hand. Sam closed his fingers around the money. Bewildered by Jesse's sudden impulse to leave he stood still and stared at Jesse. After a minute or so he shook his head and slowly turned around to go to the café as instructed.

By the time Sam returned Jesse had the white mare saddled. *Damn this white mare, she is so easy to spot. She stands out like a sore thumb*. Jesse impatiently fidgeted with his small amount of gear while he waited on Sam.

Sam returned with a large white cotton sugar sack full of provisions and a small glass jug full of drinking water. Without saying a word he handed them to Jesse and just as abruptly turned and disappeared out of the back door of the stable.

Unsure about his decision to leave, he sat quietly in the saddle. Somewhere in the barn Jesse can hear the chirping of some crickets while he is trying to decide if he is making the right decision. Elsewhere in the barn there is the sound of a horse urinating the odor of the urine drifts throughout the still air of the barn.

Jesse remains in the saddle without moving. When the strong odor of the horse piss reaches his nostrils and begins to burn his eyes he decides that he has slept in a barn long enough.

Jesse kicked the horse into motion and she vaults out of the back door of the barn into the lengthening shadows of the evening. They remain behind the row of buildings that line the main street until he reaches the river. Reasoning that wagon trains may come down the main street, he then turns to be even with the end of the main street of St. Joseph.

There is not any evidence of wagon tracks. He rode upstream in hopes of finding the river crossing that the wagon trains take. A few minutes later he sees the very deep ruts cut into the soft sand by the many steel rims of the over laden prairie schooners.

That trail is going to be easy to follow. I have some daylight left. If there is a decent moon and no clouds I will be able to follow this most of the night. That will put some distance between me and the sheriff of Putnam County.

Staring intently at the rutted trail he keeps the mare at a walk until a full moon appears. The moon is covered on occasion by a dark cloud. He passes beneath a solitary cottonwood tree and is greeted by the hooting of another owl.

The wagon tracks turn and disappear into the swirling muddy water of the Missouri River. This must be a safe place to cross the river he reasoned as he urged his horse into the cold water. When the water was deep enough that the mare was swimming Jesse slid out of the saddle and hanging onto the saddle horn he dog paddled along beside the swimming horse. It wasn't long before his feet touched the sandy bank on the west side of the river. The wagon tracks were still very apparent.

There was a feeling of relief as he urged the rested white mare into a ground covering trot. Even at a quicker pace it is easy to follow the well-worn wagon trail. He is determined to put as much distance as he can between him and the sheriff of Putnam County. He reminds himself he has to stay awake and ride through the dark of night before he can even consider stopping to rest.

It is still dark when Jesse reined the mare to a halt beside a small stream of water and let her drink and rest while he opened the sugar sack to find an apple and a baked potato. After eating he stretched out on the creek bank and fell asleep.

Jesse awakened to the singing of some robins as they hop around looking through the prairie grasses for their breakfast.

The short nap had refreshed him. He caught the mare and stepped into the saddle and quickly kicked her into a fast trot. *Maybe I can catch sight of that wagon train if I ride during daylight.*

The sun is directly overhead and the wagon tracks are still very easy to follow. The morning sun has been at Jesse's back and has warmed him. Along with the food in his belly and the sun on his back his lack of sleep caught up with him. Soon Jesse's shoulders slumped and his chin dropped to rest on his chest and he began to snore.

The white mare paid no attention to the condition of her young rider and kept moving at a steady pace. She preferred the better more even footing and softer ground away from the wagon trail. Without the rider giving her directions she wandered aimlessly threw the unmarked prairie.

With a loud fluttering of wings a covey of quail rises up to take flight from the cover of the brush. The noise startled the mare. She gave a sudden jump to one side, which awakened Jesse with a start.

Jesse looked down and realized that they had lost the wagon trail. With a sigh he turned the mare around and back tracked until he again crossed the rutted tracks. He made a mental note to not fall asleep in the saddle again.

The landscape had become hilly and the top soil was thin with a rocky base underneath it. This wouldn't make very good farm ground. Jesse spoke aloud to himself. The white mare was the only one to hear him and she paid no attention.

Jesse made camp at the foot of a small ridge. There were a few shagbark hickory trees and a silver maple tree and grass for the mare and a tiny stream of clear running water. After removing the saddle and bridle to allow the mare a good role in the rocky soil he put her in hobbles and watched her start nibbling at some new grass.

He looked for a good half an hour to find a suitable spot to make his bed. There was none. Everywhere there were rocks poking up through the thin layer of soil. Jesse spread his bed roll and did his best to go to sleep. He slept poorly and awoke with a stiff neck and back from lying on the hard lumpy ground.

"I hope that you fared better than I did last night. Of course you did. You slept standing up. I wish that I could have."

Jesse looked around, studying the surroundings carefully. He saw no sign of human life. He began to feel the loneliness of the empty spaces, something that he had not felt, even when both of his parents had died. He had his sisters and uncles Frank and his family. Now there was nothing, nobody, just the grass and trees and the few animals of the prairie.

He became fearful that there might be bandits. He had nothing but a horse to steal, yet he became more alert to the possibility that someone would hold him up for the horse that he rode and leave him afoot or worse.

Some storm clouds were forming off in the distance and a wind was beginning to pick up the loose leaves that had fallen from the trees last fall. After an hour or two on the trail he had left the hill country and was in an endless appearing prairie.

There were rain clouds and lightening in the distance but other than the wind blowing harder Jesse estimated that the rain would miss him. That was alright with him.

The mare's gait was as soothing and comforting as a rocking chair. Jesse's head bobbed up and down. He fought to stay awake, but to no avail.

Falling, falling, *I am falling out of a tree. Grab a branch or something.* "Ouch, damn, that hurts. Can't get my breath" The wind has been knocked out of Jesse. With his mouth wide open he desperately sucks in air.

With his breathing slowly returning to normal, Jesse realized that he is lying on his back in a shallow dry gulch. He reaches back behind him with his left hand to explore his right shoulder. "My right shoulder hurts like hell and I have had the wind knocked out of me. What has happened?" That is more cuss words than Jesse has ever put together. Cursing was not allowed by Uncle Frank and his wife, especially with in ear shot of any of the girls.

Moving to set up made Jesse's back ache. He looked around and was relieved to see that the white mare was close by. He sat for a few minutes while his head cleared and he got his bearings.

The white mare stood not more than 20 feet away. She was in the bottom of the little gully. Her head was hanging down one ear was erect the other bent forward. If horses had expressions the mare would have looked guilty or embarrassed. She shifted her weight, favoring her left front leg.

She gingerly tried to put some weight upon the left front leg. As soon as her foot touched the ground she picked it up. The wind has picked up as the sun starts to set in the west. Jesse moved slowly toward the mare. Partly because his back and shoulder hurt and partly because he didn't want her to be frightened and have her try and limp away from him until he had examined her foreleg.

While rubbing the mare's neck Jesse spoke softly to her. She allowed him to touch her injured front leg.

"Looks like it is a sprain, but I guess I won't be riding you anytime soon."

"I'll get you out of this little gulley and then I better start backtracking and try and find those wagon ruts before this wind blows

47

your hoof prints away. I am not much of a tracker so I better get at it before it gets too dark."

The wind had already made it impossible for Jesse to see the mare's hoof prints well enough to backtrack to the main trail. He started walking west to try and find the main wagon trail before it got dark. He moved as swiftly as his painful back and shoulder would allow him to.

After walking to the west for an hour he came upon a widened area of the gulley where some small willow trees and a couple of small cottonwoods grew close to the bank of the gulley. There were branches lying on the ground that had fallen from the cottonwood trees when the trees had been struck by lightning.

There were enough smaller branches to pile up and make a decent fire. Now if the white mare had enough strength to walk that far with him leading her they would have a good place to make a night camp. It would be getting dark by the time that he retrieved the mare and they came back to this spot.

By the time that Jesse returned with the gimpy mare a full moon was peeking from beneath the clouds. The wind was still swirling the dust and loose vegetation around making it difficult to see.

Jesse found a protected area to start his fire and gathered enough dry limbs to make a small fire for tonight and some left over to have another fire in the morning.

His spirits were improved as he warmed himself over the little blaze. He twisted one way and then the other to test his back and is pleased that it seems to be loosening up. With that information he carefully extends his arm forward then to all directions to test its mobility.

"Well everything seems to be working all right." He spoke out loud talking to the mare. It was encouraging to be able to have a fire and lie down beside it with his blanket and coat. He pulled his hat down over his ears, used his saddle for a pillow, pulled the blanket and coat around him and tried to go to sleep.

When he took stock of his situation he realized that he was in trouble. His horse was crippled; they didn't have water, and a limited supply of food. Most of all he was lost. *"Other than those few things I am doing well." Jesse* chuckled to himself. Jesse slept fitfully.

Cold and shivering Jesse sat up as he came fully awake. A fine mist filled the early morning air. The sky was overcast, but there wasn't any sign of lightening or a thunder storm.

In hopes that the wood was still dry Jesse scrambled over on hands and knees in the moist earth to where he had stored the wood. There were a few sticks on the bottom of the pile that were dry enough to burn. In spite of the light mist he was able to start a fire. He was encouraged by this one small victory over the elements.

There was a break in the clouds which gave Jesse hope that the light shower wouldn't last long. A small rainbow appeared at the western horizon. A good omen.

After eating a few mouthfuls of dry biscuits and wetting his lips with the rain fall he checked on the mares injured leg. The mare nickered a morning greeting at him as he came toward her. There seemed to be no change in the leg, it was still swollen and she was reluctant to put weight on the left front leg.

I'll have to look for that wagon trail. Hopefully the rainfall hasn't erased the tracks. I need a plan. I don't want to get completely lost away from this camp site. I'll make a big loop, starting out by going back east and then south, turn to the west and back here. I will have to pay attention to where I am so that I can get back here. There hadn't been enough rain fall to make the soil muddy.

It was midafternoon when Jesse arrived back at his night camp. Everything was as he had left it. The white mare had ventured a short ways off to graze. In mid-morning the mist had ceased. The prairie birds came out and hopped around in search of worms and other edibles. A large hawk was high overhead catching the wind drafts as it kept its focus on the ground below while looking for a meal.

Exhausted Jesse sank to the ground and fell asleep. He was awakened by a man's voice calling out. "Yo, the camp, can I come in?

"Who's there? What do you want?" Was Jesse's sleepy reply.

"There are three of us, me my wife and child. Can we come in and join you?"

49

There was still two or three hours of daylight left when the man's voice boomed out over the Kansas hills. Startled, Jesse sat up and looked around trying to locate the owner of the voice while he was trying to remember where he had put the old half rusted revolver.

Unable to see the owner of the voice or locate the revolver he decided there wasn't much choice. "Come on in." He cried out as he rubbed his eyes and tried to clear his head.

Three riders emerged from a bend in the bed of the dry creek bed. They had been hidden from Jesse's view by the bend in the creek. They had two pack horses in tow.

The leader of the group was a bearded old man clad entirely in buckskins except for his boots. The boots appeared to be army issue. He was followed by a young women and the third member appeared to be a young girl in her teens. Both of the females were dark haired with light brown skin. They too were wearing buckskin clothes and they both appeared to be Indian.

All of them rode small but sturdy looking brown and white Indian ponies. The young girl was leading two heavily laden brown pack animals.

Jesse eased himself up to his feet and drew himself up to his full height. Throwing his shoulders back he hoped that he looked more mature and manly if he was standing.

He took note that the old man had left his Hawkins rifle in the saddle scabbard.

The women sat at ease astride of their ponies. Both women rode bareback with only an old heavy blanket between their exposed brown legs and the pony's sweaty coats. The old man held the reins of the horse's bridle up high with both hands to show that he didn't have a weapon in them. Both of the women also had their hands out in the open.

Taken by surprise and unprepared, Jesse was ill at ease. He stammered, "I was a sleep, didn't know that any one was around."

"We mean no harm. We were some distance from you the first time that we saw you. We noticed that you were having some problems with a lame horse. Maybe we can be of help. My wife is very good with healing men and animals. Do you mind if she takes a look at the mare?"

Jesse was at a loss as what to do or say. He just shook his head, waved a limp wristed hand at them and said, "No, I don't mind. Go right ahead."

The old man turned his head toward the two women. "Let's light down and see if we can help this young whelp." They dismounted in unison as if they were joined together.

The youngest took charge of the horses while the older woman moved slowly toward the injured mare. As she approached the mare she spoke softly to her. The mare showed no sign of fear and let the woman rub her neck.

After inspecting the injured fore leg the Indian woman straightened up, shrugged her shoulders, She explained with an economy of words. "Sprained, Yellow Flower and I will find some plants to make a poultice." Without any further comment the two women soon disappeared into the emptiness of the plains.

"So now I know the name of the girl." I said as I offered my right hand to the old man. "My name is, Jesse and what would yours be?"

Before dismounting he hesitated before responding, "I be, Isaac Jones, my wife is, Woman of the Wind, and our daughter answers to Yellow Flower."

"It has been some time since I talked anything but Indian. I may be a little slow with the white man's speak."

The old man dismounted with a quick energetic movement. He had a youthful spring to his step as he approached Jesse with his right hand extended.

They shook hands, Isaac was short and broad shouldered. His rough hand seemed to be too large for his height. His grip was so strong that it made Jesse do all he could to suppress a grimace.

When they stood facing one another Jesse had to look down at the old man's face for Jesses was a full head taller.

Isaac removed his crumbled shapeless sweat stained felt hat and revealed a full head of hair that hung almost to his shoulders.

There was more grey than brown in the wavy mass of hair. The brownish grey hair matched his full beard that hid a deeply wrinkled face. Alert bright blue eyes were set deep in his face underneath bushy eyebrows that were the same color as his hair and whiskers. The old man's manner and friendly way eased any fears that Jesse might have had about their entering his camp.

Isaac ground hitched his Indian pony and began to gather wood for a fire. "They will want to heat some of what they found to put on the lame horse's leg. We can have the fire ready for them."

With the two of them searching for dry wood they soon had a pile large enough to last them through the night and the next morning. Isaac took out a flint and some steel and soon had enough sparks to light the dry grass and leaves at the bottom of the pile of small twigs. Soon they added larger sticks and had a nice fire going.

Isaac removed a container of water from his horse and offered it to Jesse. "

Good water ain't too plentiful. Don't peer like you have had a drink all day."

Jesse grabbed at the water bottle and eagerly gulped down several swallows. When he had his fill he handed it back to Isaac. "Thanks, I really needed that. Don't know where I am going to get some water for the mare. She hasn't had a drink in two days."

As Isaac was putting the water container back in his pack he turned and studied Jesse with a stern look. "Wondered if you would come around to that. That horse won't make another day without some care and water."

"Happens to be a tiny spring just a short ride from here. The water surfaces in a small trickle and runs just a few paces down the slope and disappears into the ground again. Most folks don't know it is there unless they are like us or the local Indians. I can lead you there first thing tomorrow."

Jesse wondered what the old man meant when he said people, like us. *What were these three doing out here on the empty prairie? Was it just happen stance that they saw him? Or are they going to knock him in the head when he is asleep and take his possessions.*

That's a laugh; he has a crippled horse, a rusty gun and no food, water nor money.

Soon the two Indian women return with several plants and berries. They go to their pack and remove a concave shaped stone. They put their plants, etc. into this stone dish and with another stone proceed to grind it into a powder. Afterwards they poured this into a cup of hot water and added some sorghum to it. The sorghum was necessary to make the poultice stick to the mare's leg. Woman then applied this concoction to the white mare's sprained leg.

Woman had been bent over applying the poultice. She straightened up and wiped the sweat from her forehead with the back of her bare forearm. With confidence she said, "In few days she will be ready to ride."

While the older woman was tending to the horse the young girl had been cooking some meat over the coals. Isaac motioned toward the cooking meat, "Join us, there is aplenty."

After they had eaten Woman took care of the horses while the young girl spread a large
buffalo skin on the ground. The sun had dropped below the western horizon when all three of the Jones family lay down together and pulled a blanket over theme selves. They were soon asleep.

The old man's snoring caused his lips to flutter. Soon a small amount of drool ran down his beard. The even and erythematic breathing of both women was a good indication that they too were fast a sleep.

They sure look peaceful and harmless laying there all curled up together. I reckon I am not in much danger from them.

He found his old revolver and checked the load before he made out his bedroll close to the fire. Jesse carefully tucked it under his saddle and used the saddle for his pillow. Exhausted, he too was soon sound asleep.

Jesse's sleep was interrupted by dreams. He rolled over and tossed and turned in the night but never came fully awake. Once during the night he sat upright in a hurry because something had awakened him. He reached for the pistol as he rubbed his eyes and tried to clear his mind. Off in the distance a coyote yipped and was soon answered by another coyote in a distant location. With an audible sigh Jesse relaxed and put the pistol back under the saddle.

The camp was stirring; everyone was stretching and scratching various parts of their bodies. Isaac put a rough work hardened hand over his mouth to stifle a big yawn while he dug threw his thick thatch of hair to scratch his head with the other hand. The fire had been out for some time; yet a feint smell of the burned wood and ashes still lingered in the motionless morning air. The morning sun was just breaking the horizon as the Jones family were beginning to stir from there comfortable bedding.

After a tin cup full of strong coffee and some rather dry and tasteless corn fritters Isaac stood up. "We better get started for that spring. It will be slow going with that lame mare in tow."

He walked over to Jesse's saddle, "I'll walk, we'll put your saddle on my riding horse." He reached down and with one hand lifted the saddle up from the ground exposing the pistol lying under it.

Isaac gave no indication that he saw the weapon. "My stirrups will be way too short for your long legs. This will just save changing them to fit you." He carried the saddle with ease to his horse and without effort settled it gently on her back.

Jesse voiced a polite objection, "I appreciate that but it ain't right. No need for that. My horse is the lame one. I can do the walking." He started to say, I'm the younger one but thought better of it for he didn't want to insult the gray haired old man.

Both of the Indian women looked toward the two men. The younger one suppressed a grin. They turned their faces away from Isaac and busied themselves getting the camp ready to move.

The old man pulled himself up to his full five foot and five inches of height, and stuck out his wide chest. He sucked in his breath, "I can still out walk any man and many of a good horse."

Jesse thought that he heard the young girl hide a snicker behind her hand.

Much later in the day they stopped for a break and a bite to eat, Isaac was still walking with a strong even unfaltering stride. He had not only kept up, there were times that he would walk far ahead and then wait for the others to catch up. So far Isaac had not even broken a sweat. He turned his head and looked at the white mare. "I believe she is keeping up tolerably well."

Isaac squinted up at the sun, "At this pace we will come to the spring well before night fall."

It was midafternoon when the small group of travelers came to the top of a low hill. In the distance was a short narrow patch of grass that appeared lusher and of a darker green color than the surrounding vegetation. A trickle of cool water came to the surface and ran on top of the ground for forty or fifty paces before it once again sought to go beneath the surface of the prairie.

Two small cottonwood trees stood as sentries at the head of the springs. They had not seen any cottonwood trees for the last thirty or more miles. Jesse was amazed that that tiny little butterfly like seeds could be borne by the wind for such a distance and then land at such a likely place that they could take root and grow.

Isaac held up his hand to stop the riders that followed him. He shielded his eyes from the sun with one hand as he carefully surveyed the surrounding low hills. Satisfied that there wasn't any danger he proceeded down the gentle slope toward the spring.

Smelling the water the thirsty white mare tried vainly to pull away from her lead rope that was firmly attached to Jesse's saddle. Jesse admonished her, "Who girl, don't be in such a rush. You might hurt yourself trying to be the first one there to get a drink."

Jesse looked around; there weren't any outstanding land marks. Even if Isaac had given him directions he probably never would have found the spring on his own.

Far above them two red tailed hawks were catching wind currents and gliding effortlessly in circles looking for any sign of a meal far below them.

Limping forward the white mare was the first one allowed to get to the head of the spring and drink her fill. Jesse led her out in the thick lush sweet grass to graze while the others are quenching their thirst at the cool clear bubbling spring. He is surprised when a small rabbit jumped out of its hiding place to run away and find another place to hide. The rabbit's movement must have escaped the attention of the two hawks.

Out of the corner of Jesse's eye he catches a movement and turns his head to see a gray fox running over the crest of the hill that they had just came from. No wonder Isaac was so cautious. The fresh water of the spring attracts a lot of visitors

The riders remove their saddles so the horses can take a role in the dirt to work the sweat out of their hair. The bridles were also removed to allow the horses more freedom to graze and drink.

Isaac appeared just as strong and energetic as if he had just finished with a relaxing morning stroll. The two women wasted no time in starting to prepare their camp site while Jesse stretched out his legs while sitting in the lush grass.

Isaac was standing only a short distance from Jesse, looking at the sweet grass where the water trickled down the slight grade. He turned toward Jesse, "Whyn't you come take a short walk with me?" He kept a steady gaze upon Jesse until the youngster slowly got to his feet.

"Where we going?"

Isaac had his head down looking intently at the ground as he walked. "Jest round the edge of this little watering hole. Keep your eyes looking at the ground. There," He pointed, "See them tracks. Those are horse tracks leading east away from the spring."

"Looks like five Indian ponies went threw here. There not fresh, maybe four or five days old."

"We'll go the tuther side. Bet they come in from that direction." He pointed to the west.

They continued looking at the soft soil around the tiny stream. There were a few animal tracks and then Isaac said triumphantly, "There they is, coming from the west to water their ponies. Now the question is, are they a hunting party or a raiding party looking to steal and do mischief."

"We came from the east and I didn't see no sign. They must have cut north or somewhere else."

Isaac waved at the two women, "Hold up making camp. Just in case someone else wants to use this watering hole, let's go over yonder past the crest of the hill and find a spot for our camp."

They caught the horses and gathered up everything and within minutes were on the move. After about an hour Isaac signaled for the group to halt. They stopped in a low area between two hills. Camp would be a dry one and without any fire for that night.

Jesse put his rusty revolver under his saddle and spread his blankets. With a small smile on his sun cracked lips, Isaac looked at Jesse. "You ever fired that piece?"

Jesse sheepishly looked at the ground and quietly replied. "No sir, I haven't."

"We better take it apart and clean and oil it before any one tries to fire it. If it blew up in your face it might ruin your pretty looks." Isaac smiled and winked at Jesse.

Isaac took the revolver, unloaded it and began to inspect the working mechanisms. He handled the small parts with his rough stubby fingers as delicately as if he were a surgeon. He was concentrating on his work and yet continued to talk to Jesse.

"These pin fire pistols give you five shots but they are only a .11 caliber. It would take all five bullets to slow a man down. If you want to stop an enemy with this gun, you would have to hit him right between the eyes."

With hesitation and without looking at Jesse, Isaac spoke in a soft voice. "I been conjugating on what you aim to do when that white mare gets well enough to ride. If'n you so desire, we can get you pointed in the right direction from whence you came. We can go with you until we know it's safe for you to journey on your own."

Jesse stuck out his chin and threw clinched teeth spoke defiantly, "I don't want to go back east. I got nothing or nobody back there to see."

"Sorry, Jesse, I don't mean to upset you. I knowed that you been running away from somebody, and that somebody is a woman."

Jesse turned his head as if it were on a swivel. His eyes flashed, "What makes you think that I have woman troubles?"

57

"You were sleeping kind of troubled like a tossing and turning. Several times you called out her name in your sleep. It ain't no shame to be running from somebody or something. After all running from something is what brought me out here."

"I am just offering to help you: if'n you want our help."

Jesse was quite for a long time before he spoke, "Thanks, for the offer, let me sleep on it."

Two big black crows were hopping around beating their wings while fighting and arguing with loud caws over some moldy corn that Yellow Flower had thrown on the ground.

The raucous crowing woke Jesse up with a start. With an alarmed shout he sat upright. His shout scared the crows into taking flight. Yellow Flower was near by; she looked at Jesse and covered her mouth to stifle a laugh.

He was embarrassed after realizing the others had been up for some time he looked up at the overcast sky searching for the location of the sun. It was hiding from view beneath some dark clouds.

Jesse stammered, "What time is it?"

Isaac had just finished tightening the cinch on his Indian saddle. He walked slowly toward Jesse and came to a stop in front of him. While he was trying to think what to say he looked down at the ground. Then he looked at the sky and inhaled deeply. "Out here we have no need for time pieces. What hour it is means nothing to us. We don't need calendars either."

"You see if the sun comes up it is time to get up, if it goes down its time to bed down. The different seasons are our calendar. Those are a couple of things that make it so special to be in this land." Inhaling deeply again, "I guess the fresh air and coming and going as you please is some more reasons that I stayed here so many years."

Isaac was quite, lost in his thoughts; he stared off into the distance as if in a trance.

After several minutes he spoke again, "I been scouting, there isn't no one at the spring. We'll go and let the horses drink and graze on that good grass for part of the day."

After arriving at the springs they took the saddles and bridles off of the horses to allow them to roll and graze without restrictions. The women left to try and find some wild onions or other plants that could be added to their meals. The mother took a small bow and quiver of arrows from her pack and carried them with her.

Isaac and Jesse sat down on the soft green grass to wait for them to return.

"You said that you had been here on the plains for many years. Just how many years is that?"

After a long silence Isaac sat upright and scratched his scalp through his thick thatch of unkempt hair. He looked directly into Jesse's eyes and quietly asks in a low inquisitive voice, "What year is it?"

Startled Jesse blinked his eyes as if he was trying to understand the question correctly. "Why it's 1845" He answered.

Isaac cocked his head to one side, squinted his eyes and held his right hand out in front of him as if he were counting. "Well, give or take a couple of years it has been about thirty five years that I have been wondering this country."

Astonished and wide eyed Jesses blurts out, "Thirty five years that must have been really something that you was running away from."

Realizing that he had been brash Jesse apologized. "I'm sorry; I shouldn't have spoke that way."

Isaac was sitting cross legged with his hands folded in his lap. "You're a youngster so
it's alright. I don't mind." He slowly turned his head away from Jesse and quietly gazed into the distance. Then he turned and studied Jesse. "I think I'll tell you. I don't know as I ever told anyone what I did before I came out here and what brought me."

Western Kentucky along the Ohio River about 1810

A stout looking young man in patched handmade clothes walked along the Ohio River shore gazing into the flowing current as if mesmerized by the water. He moved with agility along the river bank with a strong sure stride light footed for one so thick and heavy through the body. The young man who appeared to be in his early twenties came here often for it was only a short walk from his father's hilly farm. Their large family tried to grub a living from the steep hills.

A river barge was tied to the short crudely constructed dock. The young man stood at the land end of the dock looking at the barge when a man stepped from behind some wooden crates that were lashed to the deck of the barge. He stepped forth and came on to the dock.

The man was holding a piece of paper in one of his dirty work roughened hands. "Yo, you, ar ya interested in helping us float this tub down the river?"

He waved the paper at the stout young farmer. "Jes sign up and we'll float ya to places that you hain't never seen. St. Louey, Memphis and the wildest of cities, New Orleans."

"It's a great way to see the country along the river's shores and get paid doing it." He held the paper directly in front of the youngster's face. "Yes sir, don't miss out on the chance of a life time to travel. Three meals a day, its hard work but you look as if you're used to that. Are ya interested?"

The young man's eyes sparkled with curiosity. He had never been more than a days walk from his home. He ran his strong stubby fingers through his thick wavy brown hair. "When does the barge leave the dock?"

The old river rat knew that the boy had swallowed the bait. Now all he had to do was set the hook. "Shortly after daybreak tomorrow morning."

He held the paper and a stubby pencil directly in front of the young man's face. "You have to sign up first." He knelt down onto the rough boards of the wooden dock and motioned for the young man to follow. He laid the wrinkled piece of paper on the dock. "What's your name, I'll jes print it on this official ship register first. Then you can make your mark."

"Isaac Jones; "Was the hesitant answer.

The sailor shook his head violently several times and spat on the dock. "Jones, Smith, hell every bugger gives me that as their name."

The young farmer gave the rough neck an almost apologetic look and softly said, "I am sorry sir; that is my rightful name, it's Isaac Oren Jones."

The barge floated the river from Uniontown on the Ohio River to Memphis on the Mississippi River. Isaac Jones helped unload the barge at Memphis. Standing on the dock he looked along the river shore in wonder at the many buildings that made up the city of Memphis. There were even more buildings on the opposite shore. He wondered why any one would need to build so many structures and how did all these people live crushed together in one small place.

That was just the beginning of his travels along the rivers. Isaac worked his way to New Orleans where he signed on as a deck hand with a paddle wheeler. The captain of the paddle wheeler plied the river trade as far north on the big river as St. Louis.

It didn't take the river boat captains long to find out that Isaac Oren Jones had more than just a strong back He was an intelligent and honest man that could be relied on. The captains that ran the river always had a good job for a man that had those qualities as well as knowing how to read and write and cipher as well as Isaac did.

Isaac was not immune to having a few pints in one of the river side taverns. He tried to stay out of fights. If a person was to be found in a pub it wasn't always possible to avoid a brawl.

Isaac also earned respect from the hands that worked the boats and docks along the rivers. On one occasion two men decided take on Isaac together to test him in a fight. One of the men ended up with a broken jaw. The other man had his face beaten so badly that both eyes were swelled shut the next day and his broken front teeth ended up remaining in the dirty saw dust on the floor of the pub.

That story got told and embellished over and over. After that no one dared to challenge Isaac O. Jones.

It had been ten years since the short broad shouldered young farmer had signed on to that old barge as a deck hand. He now was a first mate on a respectable paddle wheeler. He often took his evening meal with the captain and slept apart from the deck hands. His responsibilities included hiring and firing of the hands. This did not increase his popularity with the men.

The paddle wheeler had docked at Cairo and unloaded some freight. The morning mist still hung over the river. Deck hands had begun to pull the gang plank in when a tall buckskin clad man standing on the dock waved his arms.

"Whoa, don't pull out just yet. I want to come aboard." He shouted.

He waved a hand with some coins clasped in his huge fingers, "Can I pay for passage to Saint Louie?" He inquired in a strong deep voice.

First Mate Isaac held out his hand for the coins as he waved at the man to come aboard... "That'll be nuff" he said as she looked at the coins. "You'll havta stay on the top deck. Ain't no passengers commodations."

The engines were started and the boats paddle wheel started churning the water as the boat slowly pulled away from the dock.

They were soon on their way up river. The river was low. Isaac stood at the bow and kept his eyes on the water for any signs of sand bars or snags that weren't normally in the channel. On the bow railing hanging from a shepherd's hook was a small alarm bell.

The buckskin clad passenger came up and stood beside the first mate. "Looking for snags and bars and the like? I have been on many a river in a canoe and know of some of the dangers of being on low water. If you don't mind, I'll stand here with you and keep my eyes peeled for trouble. My name is Lebanon."

The first mate never took his eyes off of the ever changing brown river water. In response to the frontiersman he gave an indifferent shrug of his shoulders.

Neither man had spoken for two hours. Then standing up and rising up on his toes to get a better view Lebanon pointed forward and to his right. "Up ahead a hundred paces or so, looks like a dead head just barely clearing the surface."

First mate, Isaac, came closurer to Lebanon for a better angle. He nodded his head in agreement. Isaac pulled the frayed rope and rang the bell. He than gave some hand signals to the captain and the paddle wheeler slowly turned and missed the dead head by a few feet.

It was getting dark when the paddle wheeler reached St. Louis. Isaac was busy instructing the deck hands on securing the boat with the huge ropes. He had forgotten about the buckskin clad man and did not know if he had left the boat.

It was dark and there were bats flying low over the water catching mosquitoes. Occasionally you could hear a splash when a fish would break water in an attempt at catching its dinner.

With his landing work accomplished Isaac called out, "Captain, permission to go ashore? I feel a bit thirsty."

The captain responded, "If the boat is secure, permission granted. Feels like rain. Ya better take a slicker with you."

"I ain't gonna be long. I'm intending to be back on board to do my sleeping in my own bunk."

The air was heavy with moisture as Isaac stepped on to the dirt road at the end of the dock his boots sunk into the mud from a recent rain. He struggled through the mud toward a dimly lighted building. If his memory served him correctly the building was a small tavern.

Before he had reached the shelter a light rain began to fall. The pub was only a short distance from the dock. He mumbled out loud to himself, "Damn the luck, I'm going to get wet on the outside before I can wet my whistle."

He entered the dimly lit pub. The still air of the room reeked with tobacco smoke and the stench of many spilled drinks and wads of partially chewed tobacco that lay on the saw dust floor.

The broad shouldered river sailor went directly to the bar and ordered a beer. He held the smudged beer glass up and squinted his eyes at the finger prints on the mug. He took his sleeve and wiped off the rim of the glass. He then inhaled one half of the glass of beer in one long gulp. After motioning to the bartender for another he went to the back of the room near the door and pulled out a poorly repaired broken chair and sat at one of the remaining two tables with the two beers in front of him.

Looking around he saw that there were only three more patrons in the pub. Three dirty raggedly clad men sat at a table drinking. It appeared that they had been there for some time. The three men continued to drink and the more they drank the louder and more annoying they became.

The door opened and to Isaac surprise the buckskin clad Lebanon entered. He shook himself like a wet dog scattering droplets of rain water onto the dirty floor. He walked straight to the bar and ordered a whiskey. He stood at the bar with his back to the room quietly sipping on his drink.

One of the drunks saw the buckskin wearing Lebanon at the bar and pointed him out to the others. They laughed at his clothes and made fun of him.

One man raised his voice and drooled as he spat out the words. "Hey, Indian killer, ya got any scalps?" They all laughed and the next man tried hurling forth a worse insult.

"Where's your squaws? Bring em in here. Lemme take a look at them Injun women." They whooped and laughed loudly.

Lebanon paid no attention; he continued sipping his whiskey while leaning on the roughhewn wooden plank that served as a bar.

Their insults grew louder and were more insulting. One broad beer bellied drunk shoved his chair out of the way. As the chair fell over he grabbed a hold of the man next to him to steady himself. "What the hell, ain't you got no manners? We're talking at you, buckskin; you could be neighborly and turn around."

Lebanon paid no attention until he heard the shuffling of their boots as the three men got up and staggered toward him. He then turned to face them and pushed away from the bar. There wasn't any show of emotion on his face, but his bright blue eyes were shooting sparks of fire as he mentally readied himself for a confrontation. He knew that the drunks were through hurtling insults at him and wished to bring him a more physical insult.

Beer belly was the first to come close to the frontiersman. "Damn you, I'll wake ya up and make ya holler uncle before I'm done with you." He made a clumsy drunken swing of his right hand toward Lebanon's chin.

Lebanon leaned back as the closed fist whistled by his square chin. He grabbed the man's arm as it went by and turned him on around so that he was facing in the opposite direction and with both hands gave beer belly a big shove.

The off balance drunk stumbled and fell to the floor, dazed and confused as to what happened he lay there trying to clear his head.

With fists flying the other two drunks jumped in. To give himself more room Lebanon stepped away from the plank bar. With his eyes bright and alert, he ducked and weaved and threw straight hard punches back at the two drunks.

Isaac quit drinking and sat his dirty half empty beer glass down and stood up ready to jump into the fray if Lebanon needed help. He smiled to himself, *doesn't look like he is going to need any help. Those drunks are the ones that are getting the worst of it.*

Just then Beer belly struggled to his feet and took some stumbling steps to circle around behind the frontiersman. Isaac was startled to see that he was fumbling at the handle of a large knife that protruded from its leather sheath.

The farm boy turned river boat sailor moved with a quickness that was deceptive for his short muscular frame. He came up behind the drunk. Just as the fat man's knife cleared the sheath Isaac hit the drunk in the side of the head with a powerful swing of his closed fist. Beer belly dropped to the floor out cold.

At the same time Lebanon's big fist landed squarely on the jaw of one of the other drunks. The drunk's knees buckled as his whole body went limp and he sagged to the floor like a wet blanket.

The third drunk saw that he was all alone in this fight. With nose bleeding and a split lip he turned and ran toward the door and disappeared into the rainy night.

Isaac looked at Lebanon and grinned, "You were having too much fun, I had to get in on it" They shared a laugh.

"We better go before these two sleeping beauties wake up. I know of a German eating place where we can get a cup of coffee and something to eat if you want. Thanks for taking
care of the man with the knife." Lebanon then stooped down and picked up   beer belly's big knife.

"Best rid him of his toy, before he hurts someone with it."

At the little café they drank coffee, ate sweet rolls and talked late into the night. Lebanon spoke in glowing terms of how he roamed the Rocky Mountains and trapped for beaver.

Lebanon's long face and blue eyes had the look of one who was dreaming of their loved one. "I come down from the mountains in the spring time and trade the furs for provisions for my next winters trapping season."

That dreamy look remained in his eyes and softened the features if his long angular face. "You can't believe the beauty and serenity of the mountains unless you have been there. I really love the freedom and independence of my life."

"You have never breathed as clean air as that of the mountains nor seen such beauty."

"After trading my furs there is usually enough bounty left over to get goods, mirrors, blankets, sharp knives and sharp axes, etc. to trade to the friendly Indians. I have learned to speak some of the tribe's language and they trust me. I have also learned which tribes to stay clear of."

Isaac was fascinated, he had been thinking about leaving the river boat life. There had been too many drunks, too many fights and just too many bad characters attracted to the rivers. He longed for the simple life such he had on the farm when he was growing up.

Isaac dropped his chin onto his chest and was looking at the floor as he said in a wistful voice, "I been thinking about quitting the river life. I got some coin put back. I don't have kin left to hold me back if I were to leave the river life."

Lebanon leaned back in his chair and studied Isaac carefully. "Are you meaning that you want to try the trapping life? It's a cold and lonely life."

Isaac looked at Lebanon, with a pleading voice, "Take me along with you. Let me try it for one season." He pleaded with his hands clasped together as if in prayer.

"Lebanon, I'm strong and bright. I can learn quickly, and if it helps any I know how to read and write and cipher real well. That might help when you do your trading."

"I don't mean that you can't figure. I am just saying what I can do, please take me with you."

Lebanon leaned well back in his chair and studied the broad shoulders and strong rough hands and the bright eager look in the young man's face. He allowed himself a small smile, "I reckon we could do that." He extended his right hand to Isaac. They shook hands and begin to make plans for their departure.

With money that Isaac had saved they purchased traps, a 50 caliber muzzle loading rifle, and other necessities for Isaac to begin trapping with Lebanon. They went by boat up the Missouri River and then by canoe up the Platte and on west into the big mountains. They would set their traps in the mountain streams when the temperatures dropped and the animal's furs became prime.

Twenty Five Years Later

Lebanon stepped into the fast moving mountain stream and retrieved an empty trap. The trap had been sprung. He threw the beaver trap upon the frozen bank at Isaac's feet.

"We might as well pull all of our traps."

Isaac objected, "Why so? There is two weeks of good trapping left before it starts to thaw."

"We have more plews in camp now than we can carry out. Ain't no use in taking more than we need. What we get this morning we'll skin out. We'll just have to make room for them on the pack animals."

Isaac held up his hands in surrender, "I know, it has been such a bountiful trapping season, I just hate to quit."

There was a light new snow on the ground but it did nothing to hinder their movement as they started through the shaggy birch trees toward the next set.

When they came to their next set they saw that the trap chain was pulled tight. "Looks like we have one in this set," exclaimed Isaac with excitement rising in his voice.

They had caught and traded hundreds of beavers over the last several years but it still brought the color of excitement into Isaac's cheeks when they pulled in another beaver with a fine pelt.

It was late afternoon when the two men trudged into camp weighted down with traps and beaver. "Got to be an easier way of making a living." Isaac smiled as he dropped his heavy load of traps and beaver and wiped the sweat from his brow.

The next morning they woke up to a light snow falling. They loaded beaver plews on two of their four horses. The third horse was packed with the extra plews and the most of their camping gear. The fourth and last horse was saddled for a rider but still had bed rolls, ground tarps and two Arbuckle Coffee sacks full of dried meat. It would be a long and sometimes treacherous trip over the steep mountains and down into the lower elevations of the eastern Rockies.

Isaac looked toward the craggy mountain peaks that were hidden from view by the low hanging clouds. "Hope the weather is good on the way out of this valley. The way those clouds are hanging low it don't look too promising up there in the pass. A couple feet of new blowing snow would make it most inconvenient for travel."

A hoot owl greeted them as they arose before dawn of the next day. Both men were anxious to get on the trail over the mountain and down into lower elevations. In the distance heavy gray storm clouds still hung low, clinging to the rocky slopes of the Sawatch Mountains.

Squinting his eyes as he looked at the clouds Isaac shook his head. "Don't look like very promising weather up ahead."

Lebanon did nothing to respond as he tightened the cinch on the saddle and tugged at the straps of packs on the other over loaded animals.

They had been going uphill all day. It was midafternoon when they came to the narrowest part of the trail. There was barely room enough for a single file man or horse to pass. The trail took them up past where the aspen trees grew and even above the existence of the spruce trees. It was high enough that no trees would take root there and only the mountain sheep and marmots survived in those rocky elevations.

To their right a shear wall rose up the side of the mountain. To their left was a canyon with a two hundred foot drop to the bottom where icy water ran beneath the frozen surface of the White river. The trail at this part of their journey was extremely narrow and steep with loose rocks making very poor footing for the men and their animals. Even in good weather the trail was dangerous.

They had reached the narrowest part of the trail when without warning a fierce driving wind started blowing directly into their faces. It came down the canyon with a roar; howling like a wounded animal. Heavy sleet came with the wind. The canyon caused unusual up drafts of the wind that caused the sleet to blow horizontally so there was no escaping its cold biting fury.

The sleet stung their faces and hands and worse it hurt their eyes and made visibility almost imposable. Their beards grew heavy with the frozen sleet.

All of the horses continued forward with their heads low to the ground. They shook their heads often to try and free their eyes and nostrils of the barrage of ice that came furiously at them. Soon an accumulation of ice began to build on the rumps and top of the packs of each animal.

The sleet made the footing even more treacherous.

Lebanon was in the lead with two animals. He held up his hand to signal a halt. To be heard he yelled as loud as he could. The driving wind tried to steel his words from his lips and hurl them into space. "We better stop and clean the horse's hoofs out so they can get better footing."

Lebanon carefully worked his way past his two horses to face Isaac. "This is going to get worse. The ice will start clinging to the rocky trail and make it slippery as Old Billy Hell"

Yelling threw cupped hands Isaac shouted back, "We can't stop here, ain't wide enough to put one foot beside the other. Besides these sleet storms usually don't last for more than a couple of minutes."

"I remember a place where the trail widens and flattens out at the bottom of this down hill stretch and then it starts up again. Can't be more'n five or six hundred paces. We can rest there. Let's try for that."

Lebanon shook his head in agreement. "Let's tie the lead rope of the trailing horse to the other one's tail. That should give the rear animal a feeling of safety."

They very carefully maneuvered around the nervous horses to accomplish their work. They started feeling their way with each step and began slowly moving forward.

The sleet storm refused to let up. The footing got more treacherous as the procession inched along. The rear horse in Lebanon's string began to get nervous and fidgeted at each step that she took. The trailing horse was the most excited. Her nostrils were flared and with frightened eyes opened wide she snorted and would often pull back on the lead rope causing the horse that she was tied to falter before regaining her balance.

Isaac raised his gaze from the frozen footing to see Lebanon's trailing horse getting more and more spooked. He stopped and cupped his hands in preparation to shouting at Lebanon to suggest that they should stop when Old Billy Hell broke loose.

Lebanon's trailing horse panicked and lost her footing. It happened so quickly that Isaac didn't have time to yell out a warning.

Both of the pack horses rear legs shot out from under her toward the canyon. She went down on her side and started sliding over the edge pulling the lead horse with her. Lebanon had a tight grip on the lead horse's reins and he too was thrown off balance and slid toward the prepuce.

Without uttering a sound the two horses and Lebanon disappeared over the edge. Isaac stopped and stared with disbelieve into the void.

Isaac heard nothing for if there were any screams or other sounds from the man or animals the howling wind carried them away to be lost in the confines of the canyon walls.

Isaac dropped the reins of the lead horse and took one unsteady step toward where Lebanon had disappeared over the side. He hesitated when his foot began to slip. He then carefully worked his way to the side of his pack horse where he found the hatchet.

He dropped to his hands and knees and with the hatchet chopped hand holds in the ice. On all fours he crawled to the edge of the ledge. At the edge of the cliff he raised himself up enough to see the bottom of the canyon. He hoped that Lebanon would be lucky enough to be lying on a ledge or caught on some stunted tree that was clinging to the side of the cliff below him.

Through the windblown sleet he saw the feint image of Lebanon on his back with legs and arms contorted in unnatural directions.

Isaac remained on his hands and knees and with hatchet in hand worked his way slowly back to the pack horses. Still on all fours he began to slowly lead the horses away from the scene of the accident. The wind and sleet still bore unmercifully upon him. He came to a depression in the mountain wall.

The depression was at a bend in the trail. The depression was deep enough to give him some shelter from the ice storm. To make more room he used his hands to sweep away some loose rocks.

After preparing his place of refuge he stood up and worked his way back to the nearest pack horse and retrieved a woolen blanket from one the packs.

Lebanon had traded for the blanket. It was a small colorful tightly hand woven wool blanket. Lebanon traded for it because he liked the bright green, yellow and red colors that had been used by the Navajo women to dye the wool. It had been so tightly woven that it would shed water.

With his back to the granite wall of the depression Isaac sat down and pulled his knees up to his chest and tightened the chin strap on his floppy felt hat, pulling it down over his head as far as it would go. He then pulled the Navajo woolen blanket over his shoulders and huddled up and waited out the storm.

Sitting with his body tightly curled up in a ball he began to think of Lebanon. Tears came to his eyes and spilled over to run down his leathery wind and sun tanned cheeks. His shoulders shook as he cried unashamedly.

Eventually the sleet subsided and the wind slacked up to a modest mountain breeze. Isaac's beard had thawed and the water had run down upon the front of his buckskin shirt. He wiped at his moist cheeks and took a deep breath.

Before he stood up he thought of Lebanon again. Lebanon had ended up where he would like to be. Here in the mountain wilderness that he loved. His spirit had been among the mountains and rivers for many years and now his body would remain here.

Isaac stood up and stretched his cramped legs. His back ached and his hands and knees hurt from crawling on the hard ice.

There weren't any horses in sight, they had disappeared. He was alone with only a small blanket and a hatchet and his knife that hung from his belt.

Damned horse's ran off and left me, or else they joined Lebanon at the bottom of the cliff. What am I to do?

I'll get down to a lower elevation if I have to crawl all the way on my hands and knees. Old Hugh Glass crawled miles to safety and he did it after a bear bit away a chunk of his back.

Damned if they have seen the last of Isaac O. Jones.

He chopped at the ice on the trail with his hatchet to make hand holds as he crawled slowly forward. He made his way down the steep mountain sloop at a snail's pace until he reached a lower elevation where the sleet hadn't touched the trail.

When he realized that the trail was free of ice he stood erect. His knees back and hands ached.

His mittens and the knees in his leather pants had long ago been worn thread bare by crawling over the sharp ice and rocks. Isaac ignored the blood on his hands and knees.

With an unsteady gait he began to walk toward the plains that lay down below. He had not eaten anything since before Lebanon's fall. For his drinking water he melted snow by putting it in his hat and holding the hat full of snow close to his body until it melted.

On the fourth day he was moving through some pine shrubs along the lower elevations when he saw a brown figure laying on the ground in the sage brush. After he investigated he saw it was a beaver plews. It gave him hope that one of his pack horses was alive and he might be able to find it.

Isaac had his head bowed and was keeping his eyes focused on the horse's tracks. When suddenly he realized that there were horses and riders in his path.

He was startled to see four Indian braves sitting quietly astride their ponies in front of him. They were very young, maybe in their early or mid-teenage years. All were well muscled young men dressed in their everyday clothes. They were not dressed nor painted for making war. This didn't make them any less dangerous. Two of the braves guided their ponies to come in behind Isaac. He was completely surrounded and at their mercy.

He saw that they didn't have any guns, only bows and arrows to be used for hunting. They spoke among themselves and appeared to be curious as to why a white man was wandering around afoot.

Isaac identified them as Sioux, probably of the Oglala Tribe. He was relieved to think that they were not of the Dakota Sioux for they were a more fierce and war like people. He did not speak their language but tried to communicate with them by using sign language.

Isaac gave them the peace sign and showed them that he was unarmed. Speculating that they were hunting he motioned to them that he had in fact seen a small herd of elk grazing in a small valley. He pointed back in the direction from which he had come and signed to them it would be a short ride to get to the herd.

73

One of the young braves had leaned forward over his pony's neck and watched intently as Isaac tried to make sign. Sometimes he would nod in agreement as if he understood.

The youthful Indians had a brief discussion among themselves then one of the riders to Isaac's rear rode up and with his foot gave Isaac a shove. The young brave indicated for him to start walking.

Isaac walked for some time. His legs became weary, he had been without food and water for such a long period of time that he felt weak and light headed. Sometimes he was dizzy enough that he feared that he might fall. He stumbled often and thought that he was about to pass out.

Isaac was angry at himself for such a weakness. He had been greatly fatigued before but he was always able to continue a task until it was completed. He struggled forward, for he knew if he were unable to walk they would probably not help him but would kill him.

They finally came to a small encampment and was met by a middle aged Indian man. He called out to someone in his tepee. Then he waved the young hunters to go away and pointed toward the foothills where Isaac had said there were some elk.

Isaac sank to the ground. A women and a girl came out of their tepee. With the young girl supporting him under one arm and the women the other they took him to their tepee.

They prepared a pallet for Isaac and gave him a small amount of water to drink.
"More, I am still thirsty," croaked Isaac in a weak raspy voice.

The women shook her head no and handed him a small handful of dried berries and another of nuts. She made signs to him to eat them.

Later they gave him a small bowl of warm thin soup. He then slept.

The next day Isaac awoke to the sound of a horse neighing and voices coming from outside of the tepee. He sat up to find a clay bowl of water and a portion of dried meat lying beside his bedding.

He ate and drank, then slowly and deliberately got to his feet. He was relieved that he felt much better. He knew that it would take a few days to get his strength back and that he shouldn't be in a hurry to leave. Hopefully these people would take care of him a bit longer.

The voices from outside were gay and there was laughing. Isaac felt strong enough to go outside and try to figure out what all the commotion was about.

When he parted the flap and stepped outside the Indian woman came to his side to see if he needed assistance. He smiled at her and waved her off.

She turned away from him and pointed at three carcasses that were hanging and being butchered by more women. From their excited gestures the young braves had followed his directions and were able to kill three elk. They were pleased and grateful for his help in directing them to the elk.

FIVE YEARS LATER

Isaac trapped by himself for the first year that Lebanon was not with him. Then he decided not to trap any more and began trading with the various tribes. He purchased metal tools, knives, axe, and digging tools, anything that made life easier for the plains tribes. There were brightly colored clothes and shirts and beads for the women. Tobacco and coffee were favorites. Isaac never carried firearms or liquor to trade.

Spring finally arrived after a long hard and very cold winter. Isaac decided that he would take a wife to help with the camp and keep him warm during the cold winter nights.

It had taken him several weeks but he had traded for and carefully selected ten fine Indian ponies. The ponies were young, sound and would make good trading material to fetch him a strong young wife.

Isaac saw a wagon train that was on its way west. He joined them and staid with them long enough to have an old Dutch lady give him a hair cut and trim his long beard.

Isaac was sixty years old but he was sure that his age would make no difference and that he would make a good husband. The only thing in his appearance that would suggest his age was his hair and beard that had some stray gray strands of color running through them. Of course he had a few more wrinkles at the corners of his bright blue eyes and in his forehead, but he was sure that no one would notice them.

Isaac's age was also difficult to guess as he stood erect without slumped shoulders, his walk was swift, sure and energetic. He was still trim, without a fat stomach and with a well muscled body.

It was a fine sunny clear day in the early fall. The geese honked and flew randomly as they were just beginning to form up to fly south. The horses had not put on their wooly heavy winter coats yet. There was a definite chill in the air each night after the sun disappeared in the western sky.

Isaac approached an Indian village riding his saddle horse and with a pack horse and ten trade ponies in tow. He recognized that the village belonged to an Ogallala Sioux tribe.

In the center of the village was a small group of people. In front of them was an older man sitting on a buffalo robe in front of his tepee. An older woman stood behind him and a young woman stood beside her. The young girl had her head down and was looking at the ground near her feet.

A thin but muscular young brave came forward and inspected the girl. He pried open her mouth and with his fingers inspected the soundness of the girl's teeth. He retreated to where four ponies were tied to a small bush.

The brave's black close set eyes glowed with self importance as he offered the four ponies and two blankets in trade for the young woman. The young brave spoke in a haughty demanding tone to the father of the girl.

The young brave's tone of voice got Isaac's full attention. Isaac was not favorably impressed with what he saw and heard.

The belligerent youngster was maybe a year or two older than the girl. His body gave the appearance of a coiled spring as if he was ready to attack someone or something. His eyes had a cold and hard angry look to them. He had a thin cruel face. His narrow thin lips turned down at the corners. His name was Dog Kicker.

Isaac quickly turned his attention to the father of the girl. The old Sioux brave didn't react favorably to the offer. He was passive. The mother looked at her husband as if to say, no do not take his offer. She and the father had the features and physical build of the Sioux.

Isaac saw something familiar in the two of them. He than looked more closely at the girl. She did not have the long lean muscular frame of a Sioux. She was shorter and more sturdy in appearance. Her face was broader but still pretty. She did not appear to be a Sioux Indian.

In his memory he saw the picture of a ten year old girl and an adult Sioux woman that nursed him back to health. He was sure that these are the same people that helped him survive some five seasons ago.

Isaac stepped forward and in a strong clear voice he offered, "I would like to have a wife. I have ten young sound ponies to give you in trade for this fine woman. I know that it is not enough for such a good women. It is all I have to offer. I can add a warm red Hudson Bay blanket to put over your shoulders to keep you warm in the winter and another one for your wife's shoulders."

"I am embarrassed that ten ponies and two warm blankets is all I have to offer but I would be pleased to have this one for my wife."

The old man hesitated only a minute and then with a nod of his head he accepted Isaac's offer. He rose to his feet and motioned for the young woman to come join Isaac.

The father clapped Isaac gently on the back and stepped closure to him to give him a hug. He whispered a warning in Isaac's ear, "Beware of Dog Kicker, he is cruel and will want revenge for not getting what he desires."

Her Pawnee name was Tsakira, meaning Morning Bird. She had been stolen from a Pawnee village when she was eight or nine years old.

She and Isaac learned to love one another. The next summer Tsakira and Isaac camped in a huge field of yellow cone flowers. There a baby girl was born, she was named Yellow Flower.

Woman and Yellow Flower are coming into the camp. Woman was a slight smile as she looks at her husband and triumphantly holds up two prairie chickens.

Isaac waves a hello toward them, "The women are back. They have two prairie chickens and some onions and the like."

"Jesse, it was good to talk to you. I haven't spoken that many words in American for a long time. I am glad for the chickens, they are my favorites. Of course Elk steaks and buffalo livers are good too."

Nothing else was said by any of the group as they busied themselves getting ready for night fall and cooking the meal.

The women roasted the chickens over the red hot coals of the cooking fire. They were truly delicious. Jesse smacked his lips and nodded his head toward Woman in appreciation.

"You must be a very good hunter with that small bow and arrows to have killed these small birds. Thank you, they were delicious."

Jesse looked at Woman, "How did you learn to shoot so well?"

She said nothing but smiled broadly at Jesse and then looked toward Isaac.

"It is all right, you can talk to this young man. He will do us no harm."

In a slow halting voice Woman spoke, "I do much practice. We waste no big bullets on little animals or birds. The big rifle is used for big animals, elk, deer, and buffalo. It makes too much noise."

"That makes sense." Jesse shrugged his shoulders, "But why worry about the noise?"

Isaac looked at Jesse and in a low quite voice answered, "Over these open hills with no trees or nothing else to blunt the noise, that .54 caliber canon can be heard for miles. There might be some people that we would rather not let them know of our where abouts."

They slept well that night. The next morning after they had eaten some corn fritters for breakfast Isaac faced Jesse. " Looks like if we take it slow that white mare of yours can be ridden and we can start getting you headed back toward civilization."

Jesse said nothing. The women broke camp as Isaac saddled the horses. Jesse was slow to bridle and saddle the white mare.

It wasn't long before the small group were packed, saddled and mounted and slowly on their way east.

They had been on the trail for a couple of hours when Jesse pulled up beside Isaac. "I understand that you still trade with the Indians during the summer. What do you do in the winter months?"

"Woman was born to the Ponca Tribe of the Pawnees. We bring them much meat and stay with her family during the winter months."

It was a clear sunny early summer day. The air smelled clean and refreshing. They rode threw a stand of choke cherry bushes making a flock of quail to brake their cover and take flight in a noisy whirring of wings.

The sun was almost directly overhead when Isaac signaled for them to stop. They had stopped on the bank of a small dry waterway. On the opposite bank was a large white limped sycamore tree with a patch of green grass growing in the shade beneath it.

This brought an image flashing into Jesse's mind. He saw Rebecca resting in the shade on the soft grass beckoning to him with her outstretched brown arms. Jesse squeezed his eyes tightly shut and shook his head violently. The picture grew blurred and disappeared.

This ain't right, I can't go back. I must have more time to rid myself of these memories.

The others had dismounted and stepped to the ground while Jesse sat in the saddle, his face fixed in a frown. "Isaac," He croaked his voice hoarse with emotion, "I don't want to go back to any towns or any people back there." He motioned toward the east.

He dismounted and ground hitched the mare and walked up to Isaac. No one spoke. They realized that Jesse had something weighing heavily on his mind. They gave him time to chew on it awhile before he spat his thoughts out into words.

"I got nothing that I want to go back for. Could I stay with you folks, at least for the summer?"

With a weak smile and in a jesting voice he continued, "You have had women for company for so long I was thinking that you might welcome hearing a male voice."

Isaac took several minutes to answer, "Let me think on it." He handed the reins to Flower and began walking. He headed out into the open prairie to be alone and think.

An hour had passed when Isaac walked back into camp. He went to his horse and tightened the cinch straps on his saddle and mounted his horse. "Well all of you, lets get a move on. We need to find a good place for our night camp."

Woman followed without showing any emotion. Flower's eyes were bright and she hid a big smile from her father while she mounted her pony to follow along.

The four of them spend the summer together trading with the different tribes. Coming and going as they please on the prairies, rivers and scattered forests of the territory that Isaac knew so well.

Jesse learns tracking and hunting skills from Isaac. "It is not enough to know these things," lectured Isaac. "You must study the land, the hills and rivers and know them well. Remember where there is good water and shelter. Learn who your friends are and most important learn who the people are that you can not trust. Keep your enemies close to you."

Isaac is happy to have Jesse with them. He is like a son and they enjoy being together.

Jesse pestered Woman about learning to use her bow. She finally gave in and handed him the small bow and a handful of dull arrows. At first he was clumsy and Woman shook her head and laughed at him. Yellow Flower hid her amusement by turning her back or by covering up her grin with her brown hand.

Jesse observed the way that Woman held the bow and pulled the string taut. He copied her every movement and soon was very accurate at hitting still targets.

"That is enough shooting at bushes and pieces of bark on a bank. We will go hunting," declared Woman.

Early one morning when the dew was still clinging to the sweet grass they went hunting for cottontail rabbits. They saw a rabbit that was chewing on a blade of grass. When the rabbit saw them he started running. Jesse missed the first two rabbits that they saw.

"Sometimes they will stop running if you whistle softly. Then release the arrow," She suggested. They went back to camp with one rabbit that had the misfortune to stop running when it heard Jesse's whistle.

Jesse would take walks away from camp with Flower to pick wild strawberries or look for bee hives in dead trees. Often they did nothing but walk and enjoy the summer sun.

Jesse liked Flower she was like a sister to him. He was aware that she would steal glances his way with a soft loving look in her eyes. He did nothing to encourage her in any romantic way. Sometimes when they were out of the sight of her parents Flower would be bold and want to hold hands with Jesse. Jesse did so but he did not encourage it.

The summer went by quickly. It had been a long time since Jesse had dreamed of Rebecca.

Often Isaac did not allow them time to set up the tepee and they would sleep outside on the ground. The nights were getting colder. In the early mornings when Jesse woke up there would be a sparkling layer of frost lying on the grasses in the low lying areas.

"Darned if I slept much last night. I couldn't get warm. It makes me glad to see the sun coming up this morning to warm things up a bit."

The next night as usual Isaac and Woman bedded down on one side of the camp fire. The moon was not out and with a very thick cloud cover it was a very dark night.

It wasn't long before the quite of the night was punctuated with Isaac's snoring. Flower and Jesse always slept in their separate bed roles on the opposite side of the fire.

As soon as Flower heard her father's snoring she came to Jesse with her bed roll and lay down beside him and offered to share her blankets with him. She whispered, "We can both stay warmer if we share our blankets." The rest of the night she spent curled up within the curve of Jesse's back side.

They had slept that way for two nights when Isaac spoke to Jesse. "Let's take a walk."

They were quite a distance from the women when Isaac found a place in the long buffalo grass that suited him well enough to set down. For a long time he said nothing. He merely watched three black birds chasing and teasing a red tailed hawk as they darted about harassing the hawk.

Jesse sat beside Isaac and waited for he knew that this walk was just not for exercise and watching birds in flight. He picked up a stick and drug it back and forth in the loose dirt while he waited for Isaac to speak.

Finally Isaac turned to Jesse, "Tribes have different rules about men and women. There is one tribe that will cut the end of a women's nose off if she is unfaithful. A man who sleeps with another man's women is kicked out of the tribe and has to live on his own. Men can buy a wife and if he wants to divorce her he just puts her out of his tepee along with a blanket or two."

"I always found it kind of funny that they would call that splitting the blanket. There is one rule that I hold true too. That rule is if a man couples with a woman she then becomes his wife."

He hesitated a long time before rising. When Isaac stood up he said, "Keep that in mind." Without waiting for Jesse he turned and started walking toward the camp site.

Jesse appreciated having Flower sleep beside him as it kept him warm enough to get a good nights sleep. One night Flower put an arm over Jesse's shoulder and pressed her soft breasts against him. Jesse moved away from her.

She whispered, "Jesse, don't you like me. I like you very much. I am yours if you wish to have me" She waited quietly for a response.

Jesse sat up and took Flower's hand in his. "Sure I like you a lot. I don't know if I love you in that way. I am not sure that I love you like a man should love a woman when they get married. I guess I just ain't ready to have a wife."

Jesse's denial to Flower's advancement put some distance between them. They still got along very well together and slept close to one another while retaining a more casual relationship. Still, Jesse was aware that Flower would sneak adoring looks at him from time to time when she thought he wasn't looking.

The summer went by quickly. The fall with all of its bright colored leaves and the grasses turning brown also passed very quickly. No one asked if Jesse wanted to leave Isaac's family and return to Missouri. The north winds were blowing across the prairies and the temperatures were falling when Isaac guided them toward the big muddy river where Woman's relatives, the Ponca branch of the Pawnee Tribe lived.

They had ridden over a large stretch of land that was very flat with few or no trees on it. The winds were unrestricted as they blew across this open land.

One day they came upon a rise in the flat prairie. They reached the top of the low hill and looked down upon a long peaceful appearing valley with a shallow river flowing through it. The river had many ash, cottonwood, willows and white elm crowding its banks. On the near side of the river was a village. Many of the structures had smoke rising from the smoke holes in their roofs.

Jesse smiled to himself for that smoke meant that there is a warm fire inside those homes. He was looking forward to getting out of the saddle and settling down for the winter where it was warm and comfortable.

"That is it; that will be our home for the winter. That is the Elkhorn River; it is a good place to winter." Isaac was anxious to arrive home and he kicked his pony into a gallop.

The Pawnees seemed to be a peaceful tribe. They were friendly toward the white man.

The village was a collection of structures made of mud, sticks and animal skins. These were the homes that they occupied during the winter and spring. In the summer and fall hunting parties would venture out into the surrounding river valleys to hunt for deer and other game. The women tended gardens raising melons and other vegetables. They spent their winter days holed up in the mud and stick hovels living on dried meat, vegetables, nuts and other foraged foods.

Isaac and family had arrived at the village with one of the pack horses loaded down with two fine fat does that Isaac had shot with his Hawkins. The women of the tribe took charge of the two does and begin preparing them for a feast. Later that evening the new comers were welcomed with big smiles and hugs for the women and congratulations for the success of the men at their hunting. That night every one ate well. There was much dancing and rejoicing and telling of stories.

The feasting and celebrating was winding down when an older Indian woman motioned for them to follow her. She led them to an empty hovel and motioned for them to enter. She indicated that it was theirs. The floor was hard packed clay. The entry had an old buffalo skin hanging over the opening to be used as a door. A stone fire ring was in the middle of the room above it was a small hole in the roof to draw away the smoke. The ceiling around the hole was stained black from the smoke of many fires.

During the winter months Isaac and Woman spent a lot of time visiting with her relatives. Flower had used long stems of big blue stem grass to weave a thick mat for Jesse to use as a target when practicing with Woman's bow and arrows. If the wind wasn't blowing he would use Woman's small bow and short arrows.

One bright sunny windless day while he was practicing a young Indian brave came and stood watching Jesse practice. Jesse stopped and looked at the brave.

He was a nice looking broad shouldered pleasant acting young man. Jesse had seen him hanging around Flower. He seemed too shy to talk to her or approach her.

Jesse held up the peace sign and nodded his head as if to say hello. He pointed at his own chest and said, "Me Jesse."

The young brave replied in halting broken English, "Me Kuuruks, to white man Running Bear. You too big, too strong for

84

little bow and short arrows. Do better; kill deer with big bow, long arrows."

Running Bear left and Jesse resumed practicing. Soon Running Bear returned with a longer bow and arrows. He held them out toward Jesse and nodded his head. "You try."

At first Jesse had difficulty with the longer pull which required more muscle and had a different feel. Soon he began to hit the target with consistence. The arrows would now strike the target with such force that they would go completely through it. Running Bear nodded his head in approval. "I make one for you."

Running Bear came by frequently to see how Jesse was doing with his new bow and longer arrows. Jesse noticed that the only time that Running Bear came to see him was when Flower was there.

One day Jesse went with Flower to gather wood. "Flower, did you notice that Running Bear likes you?"

She didn't respond. "Why don't you talk to him? I think he would like that. At least look at him and give him that little smile that I have seen soften your face."

Yellow Flower said nothing and continued looking for dry fire wood. When they returned to their hut they saw Kuuruks talking to Woman.

"I'll bet he is waiting for you to come back. Now be nice and don't turn your back on him. He won't bite. "Jesse attempted to hide his smile and suppress a laugh after he had spoken. Yellow Flower hugged her arm load of wood tighter to her breasts and gave Jesse a look of disgust.

Despite her immediate reaction Yellow Flower started making her self more available when Kuuruks came by. The young brave was encouraged by her responding to his attention and noticed her coy half hidden smiles. She would favor him with glances of approval or of admiration by looking softly at him and batting her dark brown eyes.

One day Yellow Flower moved her bedding away from Jesses. He took this as a sign that she really did care for Kuuruks.

The temperatures climbed and the snow melted. An early spring was in the making. Soon the willow trees were beginning to display their buds and the red breasted robins were hopping around on the ground. The only thing missing were the refreshing spring rains. They were few and when the rain did come it was light and inadequate.

After one of those light spring showers Jesse stood with his nose in the air sniffing at the fresh and clean smell of the air. *The way that the air smells so good makes me know that it is spring time. Planting time, Right now, Uncle Frank is working hard at plowing up his fields. When Sunday comes the family will all be together for a Sunday dinner after church. Probably have fried chicken. I can almost smell it.*

I wonder if my sisters are grown women yet. The oldest one is about Yellow Flowers age. Rebecca, by now I would be a father. I wonder if it is a boy or a girl. I hope Mr. O'Toole is still with them.

Isaac shouted, "Jesse, what are you doing? Quit standing there day dreaming and get those pack harnesses ready to go like I told you to."

Isaac was unusually nervous and anxious to go and buy goods at the white settlements to trade with the Indians. They were getting their horses packed and ready for the journey when Woman stunned Isaac with a question. "Will we be taking Yellow Flower with us?"

Shocked, Isaac stopped what he was doing and turned facing Woman. "What did you just say?"

With a disgusted look she looked at him as only a wife can give to an unaware husband. "Kuuruks has been pursuing Yellow Flower and she is receptive to his advances. I am sure that he wants to marry her. She may not want to leave him here and go with us."

Isaac shook his gray head, "You must be daft. My little girl can't be ready for marriage. I ain't about to sell her to some young buck. Not for ten horses or a hundred horses. She's too young." His voice got louder and louder as he continued talking and his face turned red beneath his beard.

To calm him Woman put her hand on Isaac's shoulder. She spoke in a quiet even tone, "My husband, Flower is one year older than I was when we got married. I have never regretted marrying you. It has been good."

"It has surprised you that your little girl has become a woman. You must think about what to do."

Without answering Isaac turned on his heels and angrily walked swiftly into the emptiness of the prairie. It was several hours before he returned. He found Woman and motioned for her to follow him.

When they had gotten far enough away that no one could hear them Isaac spoke. "I see that you are right. She is a woman and is old enough to be married. It just seems so sudden. Not long ago she was learning to walk and ride a horse."

His eyes were misty with tears. "What do you think we should do?"

Women took Isaac's strong rough hand in hers. "Let us talk to her. Tell her that we have seen that there is a man in her life. We will take her with us to buy trade goods and then go trade them. When that is done we will come back here. That maybe our last trip that we take with her. It will give us some time with Yellow Flower. Then if they are to get married they can do so when we come back. It shouldn't take us more than two or three full moons to do that. They will have to be patient for a short time."

They spoke to Kuuruk and Yellow Flower of their plan. Both of the young people smiled and nodded in agreement. They would marry upon the families return.

Isaac made it clear there would be no need for a dowry.

They told Jesse that they were going to a white settlement to buy trade goods and asked him if he wanted to go along. If he liked the settlement he might choose to stay. If not he was welcome to remain with them.

Soon the family and Jesse were on their way to the white settlement. Very little rain had fallen and their ponies kicked up clouds of dust as they walked along the trail. Some of the bunch grass that grew on the rocky hill sides was stunted and unhealthy looking from the lack of rain.

A soft breeze was blowing from the south west. A few darker clouds were pushed along by a light breeze.

Without warning Woman turned her pony toward a near by low hill. She kicked her pony into a gallop and when they reached the crest of the hill she reined her horse to a sudden halt. There she dismounted and tied the pony to a small button bush.

She stood on the hill top as if in a trance. Facing east she raised both arms out in front of her and began to chant. Woman slowly turned to the north and after some more chanting she turned to the west. With arms still extended her chanting became louder as she finally pivoted on her moccasins toward the southwest.

With the light breeze blowing in her face and her arms still held out in front of her the rhythmic sing song chanting grew louder and louder. The harder the wind blew the louder her chanting became. The ever increasing force of the wind caused her black hair to flow out behind her. Her Elk skin skirt was lifted up by the wind to expose her brown thighs.

Finally Woman lowered her arms, stopped her chanting and sprang onto the back of her pony. She rode down the hill at a full gallop and jumped from the ponies back in front of Isaac.

"Quick, there is wind and lightning coming. We must find a safe place to get away from the lightning."

Jesse looked at the southeastern sky. Although the sky was getting darker he did not see any lightning in the clouds.

Isaac knew he should not question her. "Be quick, we will go to that dry creek bed. Bring the pack horses and stay away from those trees that line the banks of the creek or there will be Old Billy Hell to pay. Especially that big cotton wood, lightning is partial to cottonwood trees."

Without questioning him the women hurried to follow Isaac's orders. Jesse looked at the partially cloudy sky and didn't see any need to get so excited.

They were at the bottom of the draw and had just finished hobbling the horses when they heard the first muffled clap of thunder rumbling in the distance. Isaac unpacked two large buffalo robes,

"Turn these hide side out and cover yourselves with them. They will keep the rain off and be protection if it hails. Stay low and for God sakes don't stand in any water."

Although the wind was increasing in strength Jesse still doubted the need for all of this precaution because of some arm waving and chanting that Woman had done. His doubt was erased when he looked to the southeast and in the distance saw the first small hail stones bouncing off of the dry earth. He hurried to kneel down and take cover under the buffalo robe with Yellow Flower.

Lifting the edge of the buffalo robe Jesse peeked out to see the sky lit up with bolts of lightning flashing brilliantly directly above them. The lightning bolts were immediately followed by the sound of thunder booming like cannon fire. The storm had moved to where it was directly over them. Jesse hurried to get back under the protection of the buffalo robe.

He wasn't too soon in seeking cover. The hail hurled down on their skin fortress with a vengeance. The hard stones of ice made a tinny sound as they hit the tightly stretched skin shelter.

The hail storm lasted only a few minutes. Soon after it had ceased they heard Isaac calling out that it was safe to come out from hiding. The ground was covered with a thin layer of small hail stones. The hail sparkled in the daylight like millions of little jewels.

When they emerged from underneath their temporary cover they saw that one large limb of the cottonwood tree had been split by the lightning. It dangled dangerously close to the ground at the base of the tree.

Scratching his head in amazement, Jesse was dumb founded, "What was that all about?" He looked at Woman. "How did you know it was going to storm like that?"

Isaac laughed, "Ain't that wife of mine something. She got some kind of strong medicine. That is why we changed her name to Wind Spirit Woman."

"She just feels the change a coming. She don't make it happen, just knows it is about to happen. We don't tell any of these wild Indians that she can do this. They are spirituous enough that they

89

would think that she controls the wind and the storms. Ain't like that; she just can tell when they is a coming."

"Some of these heathens might think that Woman is a witch with big medicine and evil powers. No telling what they might want to do to her so I just stay quiet and call her Women."

"Let's saddle up and get to the settlement before dark. We can get our trade goods and get on the trail sometime tomorrow."

By the next afternoon they were on the trail headed west. Their pack animals were loaded down with warm blankets, shiny trinkets and various kinds of metal tools that the Indians desired. They had many sharp metal knives, axes, awls, fish hooks and other tools to replace the Indian's primitive stone and bone cutting tools. On this trip Isaac had decided to take to two Springfield flintlock rifles with them for trade. In addition he had packed enough black powder and fifty balls for each rifle.

Jesse turned in the saddle and faced Isaac. "Where are we headed? What is our destination?"

"We might make it to Crow country, along the Tongue or Powder River. They are a tribe that is friendly to the white man and they usually have lots of beaver plews for us."

"Maybe we will stop off near the Wind River and trade with the Arapaho. They's about the same friendliness to whites. Course if we do that we have to hide the women. Those Arapaho hate the Pawnee."

"A lot depends on this drought. If it is dry all the way west we may not travel as well. The wild game will not be in their usually feeding areas. The dried up water ways will also be a problem."

"Then there is the Indians, they will have to range out of their normal territories for grazing for their herds of ponies. It is going to be harder to find the buffalo and deer that won't be in the usual feeding grounds."

"The tribes have unmarked boundaries and there is often disputes when these boundaries are violated. Ain't no written down rules, but there is generations of tribes that know where they should and shouldn't go."

For five days they had kept up a steady pace following along beside the Platte River. They came to an area where a small tributary joined the Platte from the north. Isaac called a stop to their procession. They were on the top of a hill looking down a high steep bank at the junction where the two rivers became one.

Long ago an oak tree had lost its grip in the loose soil of the bank and had fallen over. The roots stuck up out of the ground with the length of the tree lying on its side parallel to the top of the bank. Many of the branches had rotted away or been broken off to be used for firewood. On top of the bank were many stone fire rings where travelers had helped themselves to the easily reached broken limps of the fallen tree.

Isaac dismounted and stood at the top of the long bank directly above the downed tree. He removed his old felt hat and let the south breeze blow threw his graying hair.

He pointed down at the little stream that was entering the bigger Platte River. "That little river has some good brush cover and some sweet grass growing back away from the river. There's a stand of willows in there that the deer like to bed down in."

"I have hunted that place many a time and I ain't never failed to get a deer of some kind out of there. You people dismount and take care of the horses. I'll take my Hawkins and ride down there and see if I can scare up some unsuspecting critter. We been on the trail for five days and my mouths a watering for some fresh meat."

"The wind is behind us and blowing toward the cover, so I'll go to the west and circle around. I'll then come down threw that cover with the wind in my face that way any critters that are in there won't get my scent. There is a little game trail beside the little river. I'll come out on it."

Isaac checked his rifle and coaxed his horse over the edge of the steep bank. They started off down the long steep bank at a fast pace. His horse was slipping and sliding as they went down the treacherous footing on the side of the steep bank.

Woman watched her husband turn his horse to the west and ride for one half mile before they crossed the Platt River to circle around and enter the area that he wanted to hunt.

She shook her head, "The way that he pushed that horse down that steep bank, he thinks he is still a young man."

The two women begin placing wood in one of the fire pits while Jesse unsaddled the horses to allow them the freedom to role in the dirt. The wind was increasing and was blowing the dust and sand along the ground. The dust was getting in their eyes and noses, making breathing difficult.

When the strong wind blew a tumble weed into Woman's legs she decided. "We can't build a fire up here. We will have to camp down below near the river's edge. Leave the ponies up here while we move our gear down below. This wind is getting stronger and will blow our gear away if we aren't careful."

They had just begun to pick up their gear when they heard the muffled sound of a shot. "I bet that is Isaac's, we'll have meat tonight." Jesse exclaimed with excitement as he rubbed his stomach.

They stopped to pick up their gear when they heard the sounds of men screaming. They were terrible high pitched sounds coming from more than one person.

"Those weren't Isaac's yells, they were cries of Indian warriors." Woman screamed, "Isaac, Isaac, he is in trouble." She started to run toward the crest of the steep bank.

Jesse grabbed her by the arm, "We can't get there in time to do him any good and we don't have any guns ready to fight with. I got this one little pistol, that's all."

In an attempt to hold her back Jesse wrapped both of his arms about the struggling woman. Yellow Flower shouted. "Mommy, look down below!!!"

Riding at a gallop six warriors came out of the brush. They pulled to a halt in a cloud of dust. One warrior was dragging a body behind his pony. He rode forward to the river's edge. He looked up the hill toward Jesse and the two women and shouted an obscenity as he shook his free hand at them.

Woman cried out in anguish, "It's Dog Kicker, he has killed Isaac; Isaac, my husband."

Dog Kicker had a rope around both of Isaac's ankles and had drug him through the dust. He wanted to gloat of his deeds in front of Woman. She was the woman who had spurned him as a husband many years ago.

"Good God, what have they done to him?" cried Jesse.

Isaac's body had been mutulated; the cruel and ruthless Dog Kicker had cut him open from his crotch to his breast bone. Then he had dragged the body along in the dust until his intestines became strung out behind him for several feet. That wasn't enough of an insult for the heathens. They had cut off Isaac's privates and stuffed them in his mouth.

The six warriors were yelling and waving their weapons and gesturing toward the onlookers at the top of the river bank. They screeched and yelled while holding their weapons over their heads. Jesse could see that there was only one of them that had a rifle.

Jesse put his hand around the grip of the small revolver that he had in his waist band and yelled at Flower. "Quick, take your mother, get behind that old downed tree. Take her bow and arrows, get a hatchet, something to protect yourself with. Hurry!!!!" He was running for cover behind the downed tree as he yelled at the two women.

Jesse and the women had barely reached the fallen tree when five of the warriors began their charge up the river bank. Yellow Flower was on the left gripping a sharp metal hatchet. Woman, with tears staining her cheeks clenched her teeth as she looked down the hill at the horrible sight below. She prepared to defend herself by laying three arrows on the log and then notched a fourth into her bow. Jesse had his small caliber revolver in his hand and waited on the right of the two women.

His only weapon was the light caliber revolver and the hunting knife in his belt. He had briefly thought about the long bow and arrows that he had tied to the back of his saddle. He knew that there wasn't enough time to find and unpack the bow.

Dog Kicker's bragging had barely given them enough time to take cover. He held the rope that was tied around Isaac's lifeless ankles with one hand and with the other hand motioned for the five warriors to charge up the river bank and attack Jesse and the two women.

The wind was blowing into the faces of the charging warriors and their horses as they came up the steep bank of the river. The wind had increased in velocity and was swooping down over the crest of the bank with gale force carrying tumble weeds, dust, dirt and small pieces of loose debris into the faces and nostrils of the warriors and their horses.

The Indian pony's eyes became red and irritated by the blowing dust and it clung to the moisture in their nostrils making breathing difficult. The dust blowing into the horses eyes made them balk and chomp on the bits that their riders used to control them. The spooked mounts made it difficult for their riders to control them long enough to get off any accurate shots.

Above the war whoops of the charging Indians Jesse heard a shot being fired by the one musket bearing Indian. Most of them were having trouble getting their mounts to behave long enough to charge up the bank into the blowing sand.

Jesse saw the horse of the rider that was directly in front of him stumble and go to the ground pitching his rider off. The pony quickly scrambled to its feet and turned to run back down the river bank. In falling the rider had gotten his arm tangled in the reins and he was being dragged down the hill by the panicked pony.

Knowing that his small caliber pistol had a very limited range Jesse fought the urge to fire it prematurely. The warrior that was the furthest to his right had jumped off of his spooked pony and was only a few feet from Jesse when he fired a shot and hit him in the chest. The warrior didn't seem effected by the bullet and never broke stride. Jesse fired two more shots as quickly as he could pull the trigger. The Indian stumbled forward and fell ramming his head into the oak log.

Without hesitation Jesse turned to the next warrior. The Indian had jumped from his charging pony and was preparing to leap onto the log. This time Jesse held the pistol at arm's length and aimed for the man's head. He squeezed the trigger and saw a dark spot appear in the middle of the warrior's forehead. The force of the dead Indians charge carried him over the top of the log and past Jesse.

While Jesse was occupied with those two, Woman had released an arrow into the neck of the warrior that had fired his musket from the bottom of the river bank. The arrow had struck him a fatal blow while he was still some distance from their oak fortress.

Women quickly notched another arrow and just as quickly released it, in a blur of motion she did this three times. All three arrows found their mark and were protruding from the ribs and shoulder of the remaining charging warrior. The small arrows didn't have enough force behind them to penetrate deep enough to stop the strong broad shouldered warrior. With the small arrows still in his body he leaped from his horse and vaulted the log.

Woman grabbed the hatchet that had been in Yellow Flower's hand. She aimed for his head and swung the hatchet as hard as she could, while Jesse beat the warrior over the head with his empty pistol. Within a few seconds the warrior slumped to the ground with his scalp bleeding and the arrows protruding from his body.

Jesse grabbed onto his hair and pulled him up and slid the big warrior over the side of the log. His lifeless body rolled a few feet back down the steep bank.

Jesse and Woman straightened up and looked at one another. They were both sweating and had the blood of their enemies splattered on their faces and chests. Suddenly Woman leaped over the log and taking the skinning knife from her belt she deftly removed a warrior's scalp. She held it up in her left hand and shook it at Dog Kicker while she screamed. "We are wind warriors. I'll come get your scalp next, you son of a dog."

Jesse became alarmed when he realized that Yellow Flower had not moved nor spoken. He went to her. She was lying on her back in the dirt. There was a dark hole in the front of her Elk Skin dress. He stared down at her in silence and watched as the dark stain on her dress got bigger and bigger.

95

He turned and yelled, "Woman, Woman, it is Yellow Flower. She is wounded, come quickly."

Woman dropped her knife and the grisly prize. She leaped over the log and held Flower in her arms. Flower had her eyes closed and her chest was motionless. She was not breathing. Her arms lay limp by her sides.

Woman pulled her daughter to her and stroked her black hair. She whispered in an emotionally hoarse choked voice. "No, No, Why her, she is so young. I would gladly take your place if you could live." Woman looked up at the sky. "Tirawa Atius,(Father Above) why didn't you take me?"

Woman moaned and cried and rocked back and forth while she held Flower tightly to her. She continued to mumble, "No, No, this can't be. My family is gone." She wailed in her grief.

Jesse didn't know what to say or do. He stood up and looked down where Isaac's mutilated body lay in the dirt along the river bank.

He put his hand gently on Woman's shoulder. "You stay here. I'll go down and take care of Isaac."

Jesse was at the crest of the bank when he had a strange sensation creeping along the back of his neck. He thought someone must be watching him. Cautiously he looked under every bush and behind every tree that might be hiding an enemy. All of a sudden he realized what was different.

The air was still and quite, there wasn't a breath of air moving. Shortly after the fight had ended the wind had stopped blowing.

Jesse reached the packs that were lying on the ground and knelt down on his knees to untie two blankets from the packs. His hands trembled and his shoulders shook as he allowed himself to break down and without restraint he cried. After a few minutes he spoke out loud to himself, "Get a hold of yourself. I got to be a leader now. There ain't no one else. Woman and I will have to work together. She may not be much use for a while."

Later Jesse stood over Isaac's body and swallowed hard while trying to contain his emotions. The bitter taste of bile rose up in his throat when he looked at what had been done to Isaac. The excess

96

amount of saliva in his throat was a warning that he was about to throw up. He was desperate to try and hold his stomach contents down so he began swallowing hard and fast.

It's best if I clean Isaac's face off first. Then I'll try to put him back together a little bit.

He went to the river and wet the corner of one of the blankets and began to clean Isaac's mouth and gray whiskered face. Again he choked back the saliva and bile when he placed Isaac's intestines and other parts on top of his body. Jesse used the rope that had bound Isaac's ankles to tie the two blankets tightly around his lifeless body.

Standing erect Jesse studied his work. He spoke out loud, "Well, old man, I guess that is going to have to do. I didn't know you very long but I learned to love you."

Looking up the river bank he saw that Woman still cradled Flower's still life less figure in her arms. He started walking to search for Isaac's Hawkins and his horse.

He had walked only a short distance when he saw a dead deer lying in the brush. Isaac had laid his Hawkins Rifle down with the barrel resting on the front leg of the deer. Not far from the deer were the tracks of several horses and a few spots of blood stained the dusty soil in the narrow trail. That would be where Dog Kicker had caught and tortured Isaac before dragging him to the river's edge.

Now, if I can find his horse I can haul poor Isaac's body up the hill. Later I'll come back and get the deer.

The horse was not far away. The yelling and screaming of the Indians had made her nervous and spooked. She trembled and her nostrils were flared open and eyes alert as her ears were cocked forward. She was ready to bolt. Jesse took his time approaching the mare until she calmed down enough for him to lead her to Isaac's body.

Wind Spirit Woman was still holding her daughter tightly in her arms and she was wailing in a high pitched death chant.

"Woman, I have Isaac's body here. What are we to do with them? They will have to be buried."

97

Several minutes went by. "Woman, it will be dark soon. We must make camp and you can think about what you want to do with Yellow Flower and Isaac's bodies."

Later a light breeze sprang up and began stirring the leaves on the trees and causing the grass to gracefully bow in its surrender to the winds efforts. Jesse started a fire and laid out bedding on the ground. Exhausted he laid down to sleep.

In the early light of predawn Woman shook Jesse's shoulder. "We will make a travois and take both of them back to where my people live. That will be their final resting place."

Woman's pale face sagged, and her eyes were dull and lifeless. She apparently had not been able to sleep.

Several days had passed since the Indian burial procedure had taken place back in the Pawnee village. Wind Spirit Woman had not been eating or sleeping well. Sometimes in the middle of the night she would get up and leave the hut. She carried her heavy burden of grief outside to share it with the birds and animals of the night. Jesse could hear her groaning and crying in the darkness.

She did not look well and did not take interest in anything. Her relatives surrounded her with love and affection and shared in her grief. They tried to comfort her still she seemed distant and talked to no one.

For safe keeping Woman and Jesse had stored Isaac's trade goods inside of the hut with them. One day Jesse was bent over checking on the rifles and powder to see if they had remained dry when Woman came up behind him. "We should take those and trade them. That is what my husband would have wanted. We will leave here in two days."

It has been several weeks since they had left the Pawnee village with the trade goods packed on two strong young ponies when they crossed into an area that was known to be part of the Crow Indians hunting grounds. Although the Crow were friendly to the white eyes they were not always so with The Pawnee. Jesse and Wind Spirit Woman were very cautious in their traveling, staying to the least traveled trails and camping without lighting a fire.

In the early morning as the sun was just barely over the horizon they were surprised by four unexpected visitors. Four young Crow braves gave warning before they rode into camp. They immediately signaled that their intentions were peaceful.

One brave rode forward a few paces from the other three. He made a sweeping motion with one hand at them. "You, the killers of four Sioux warriors?"

Woman and Jesse wondered if they admitted to killing them that it was going to be a reason for the young braves to attack or if they merely wanted to know the answer.

Woman stepped forward, "It was my husband that Dog Kicker tortured and killed. When they attacked us they killed my daughter. We killed the four of them when they attacked us." She defiantly looked at the young man with her eyes blazing and her chin held high. "If they would not have attacked us I would have tried to kill all of them for killing my husband."

Women was not through, "I see that you are Crow, why do you care what happens to some lowly Sioux who fight with old men and women?"

It was not proper for a woman to speak to a brave in such a manner and especially not about making war. The young brave did not seem disturbed by Woman's outburst. "My chief sent us, He will allow you to pass through our hunting grounds and trade as you please, even though you are a woman of the poor mannered Wolf People Tribe."

"My chief says this is so because you and the tall white one are great warriors with much strong medicine. It is also so because the trader with the gray beard was our friend."

He turned his horse and started to ride away. Suddenly as if he had forgotten something he stopped. Turning in his saddle and looking over his shoulder he spoke. He pointed to the west. "A few days ride in that direction is where Dog Kicker has camped. His camp is near the small creek that runs beside a lot of the rough barked trees." He kicked his pony in the ribs and they rode off at a fast gallop. Their horse's hooves kicked up dirt and frightened some quail to take flight from their hiding place in the sage brush.

It had been a week since Woman and Jesse had talked to the Crow hunting party and learned that there was a Sioux camp on the western border of their territory near the Pawnee River. They were sure that Dog Kicker was a member of that camp.

After hearing that news about where Dog Kicker was camped; Woman could only think of killing Dog Kicker for what he had done to her husband and daughter. She barely ate and rarely talked to Jesse unless it was to plan on how to sneak up on her enemy and kill him.

They rode toward the Sioux camp. During the last four days their horses had been climbing a gently sloped grade that was getting gradually steeper each day. It was getting later in the fall and there was a crisp chill in the air. The choke cherries were ripe on the bushes and the grass was turning brown. Geese were forming up to find their strongest fliers to lead the V shaped formation on their long flight south.

On the morning of the eighth day they came across many fresh tracks of unshod Indian ponies. They knew that they were very close to the camp as the horse droppings were soft and smelled very fresh. The tracks were leading them toward a small valley. Woman remembered camping and hunting there with her family.

"The old camp site is not far. A small clear stream runs there, and there is good grass for the horses a long the banks." Woman spoke as she dismounted. "We should leave the horses and scout over that rise. She pointed toward the grassy crest that was about a mile away."

There was a small copse of pine trees near by where they tethered the horses so they could graze. They started walking toward the crest of the hill. Jesse took the Hawkins rifle and Woman had her small bow in her hand with a full quiver of arrows slung over her shoulder. In addition both of them carried a razor sharp Green River Knife in a sheath at their side.

They hadn't gone far before they saw the smoke from several fires lazily drifting upwards in the still morning air. The smoke curled up just above the crest of the hill.

They dropped to the ground and began to proceed on their hands and knees until they could see the tops of some tepees. They then dropped down on their bellies and slowly wormed their way forward threw the tall dry buffalo grass until they had a clear view of the little valley below.

They were surprised to see only a half a dozen tepees. "Not a big war party, probably just came to hunt. The game come here often, deer, even buffalo. Sometimes the geese land on the small creek," whispered Woman.

As they watched the entrance flap of the tepee closest to them was opened and a man emerged. He went to the end of the tepee and made water. He then turned toward them and looked directly at the two of them. They pressed their bodies and faces into the dry earth. The man yawned and turned to go back inside.

"That's him that is Dog Kicker." Woman whispered as she pressed herself deeper into the buffalo grass and the loose sandy earth.

Without speaking they began to push themselves away from the crest of the hill. Once they were far enough away from being detected they stood and ran in a crouch toward the horses.

Both of them were breathing heavily as they untied their horses. Jesse stopped moving with the bridle reins in his hands before mounting he turned to Woman. "Why didn't you let me shoot Dog Kicker? He was an easy target standing there in the open with his hand holding onto his privates."

Woman had grasped her pony's mane and swung her leg over the ponies back. She hesitated speaking. Woman looked down at Jesse and with fury in her eyes and threw clenched teeth she growled, "I want to kill him myself." With an angry kick she made her pony lurch into a fast gallop, stirring up the dust as she rode toward higher ground.

Jesse mounted his pony and rode after Woman at a slower pace. He didn't wish to stir up more dust for fear that someone would

101

see it. Soon Woman slowed down and allowed Jesse to catch up. She spoke without looking at Jesse, her jaws were clenched and her face was still contorted in a mask of hate. "I need to get to higher ground to contact the wind gods."

They rode until they came to a promontory of rock. After they had dismounted, Woman handed the reins of her horse to Jesse and without speaking she begin to climb to the top of the rock formation. Once at the top she fell to her knees and with her shoulders slumped and her head bowed she remained that way for a long time.

Finally Woman stood up and with her eyes closed she went into a trance, holding her arms and face up toward the sky her jet black hair fell upon her shoulders behind her. She faced the east first and then turns slowly to face in different directions. She is like a human compass needle that is searching for the wind direction and the weather.

Woman stops and faces to the northwest and stretches her arms and face skyward. She begins to chant, after about an hour she lowered her arms and carefully climbs down the rocky slope.

"The wind will blow hard from the northwest tonight. There will be thunder and lightning. We will wait here so as not to be seen. Then we will go back before sunset and wait on the hill top for the right time."

That evening she again stands with arms and face turned upward. "It is time we must go to the crest of the hill now. Heavy black clouds will cover the moon and it will become very dark and no one will see us. Take our horses with us."

Dark storm clouds began rolling and churning in the sky. In the distance bolts of lightning pierce the air. The wind from the northwest is increasing in intensity as they approach the small copse of pine trees below the crest of the hill. The early darkness will be cover for their movements. Woman doesn't hesitate; she boldly rides to the crest of the hill and dismounts.

She motions for Jesse to follow her. It is early in the evening but as dark as midnight and the wind has picked up in speed tearing up sand and dust and anything loose in its path. It is pitch black and with the wind at their backs they walk down the slight incline toward the tepees.

They are a mere forty paces from Dog Kicker's tepee when Woman signals for them to stop. She notches an arrow in her bow and lays two more arrows down on the ground in front of her. Turning toward Jesse she nodded her head, "call the cowardly dog out here to fight you. Call him names, anything to get him to come out so that the wind and dust will be blowing into his face."

Woman drops to one knee with her bow strung tight while Jesse begins calling out insults in a loud voice. "Dog Kicker, come out and be prepared to die. I am here to kill you for killing Isaac Jones. Come out and fight me face to face. Just the two of us. Do you kill only old men? Are you too scared to face a young man? Prove that you are a warrior. Come out of your tepee and fight me."

Jesse yelled as loud as he could.. He had a tight grip on his sharp knife and Woman was ready with her bow. Jesse and Woman did not have to wait long.

The tent flap to Dog Kicker's tepee was flung open and he stepped out into the wind and dust with a war hatchet in his right hand and a knife in his left one. He ducked and turned his head away from the gale force wind to shield his eyes from the dust. Squinting into the wind he tried to locate his enemy.

Woman cried out, "Charge him now, before he gets his bearings."

In the tepee across from Dog Kicker his neighbor, Bad Foot, heard the yelling over the noise of the wind.

Bad Foot had been born with a crippled foot. He was unable to run and play with the other Indian boys. Besides having a crippled foot he was rather small with narrow shoulders and hips.

Bad Foot hated his name but he never voiced his dislike. Realizing that he would not be able to make war or steal horses he decided to be good at other endeavors. He learned how to track animals and men and was soon one of the best trackers in his tribe. With that information he studied the habits and movements of game, from the small rabbits to bear and buffalo.

Bad Foot became an excellent hunter and his family never went without meat. Being an excellent hunter was not enough. As he got older Bad Foot desired to have a wife. The desirable young women were not interested in the small crippled young man.

Since he could not steal horses he did not have anything to buy a wife with. Fathers who had desirable daughters sold them to the highest bidder.

Bad Foot then settled for marrying Turtle. Turtle was slow in thinking. This seemed to make her rather slow in her work too.

Many of the Indian husbands would beat their wives when they were displeased with them. Bad Foot had patience; he never beat Turtle nor made fun of her.

Turtle and Bad Foot had been married for three summers and they didn't have any children. Bad Foot wanted a child. He had mounted Turtle many times during each moon cycle without her getting with child. In order to father a child he wished he had a second wife.

He coveted Doe Skin, who was Dog Kicker's youngest wife. She had soft skin like a young doe. Her breasts moved pleasantly under her dress when she breathed hard and she had a full firm butt. Even as nice as she was Dog Kicker would beat her often. When Dog Kicker's tepee was set up close to his Bad Foot was able to see these bad things with his own eyes.

Now the wind was blowing very hard yet Bad Foot heard voices calling out from somewhere outside. He pulled aside the entrance flap to the tepee, bending over he left just enough room to peek outside into the wind and dust. The moon was covered by very dark black clouds and lightening sprang out from the heavens and lashed at the ground below.

There in the dark when there was a bright flash of lightening he was able to see a figure with a war hatchet in his right hand, crouched forward so that the wind would not blow him away. Bad Foot was sure that the person was Dog Kicker. He held his left hand up to shield his squinted eyes from the windblown sand and dust.

Bad Foot was fearful that their small hunting party might be under some kind of attack by an enemy. He started to close the flap and go get a weapon to defend himself when through the haze of darkness and dust there was a flash of lightening. He saw Dog Kicker suddenly straighten up and drop his war hatchet.

It was then that he could just barely make out through the wind and blowing dust; what looked like an arrow in Dog Kicker's chest. Dog Kicker reached for the arrow that was imbedded in him. Before he could tug at the offending arrow two more arrows pierced his body in quick succession. They had been shot so quickly that they seemed to come at the same time. With a scream of rage Dog Kicker dropped to his knees.

Bad Foot was frightened, but before he could straighten up there was another flash of lightening that allowed him to see a figure being carried by the strong wind toward the fallen Dog Kicker. He wasn't sure but it appeared to be a tall white man that bent over the fallen Dog Kicker. Because of the blowing dust he could not see too well but he recognized by the movements that the man over Dog Kicker had grabbed his hair in one hand while the other arm made a quick slicing motion. Bad Foot recognized that as a motion that is taken when one cuts an animal's throat. In this case it was Dog Kicker's throat that had been cut.

While still holding tight to the fallen enemy's hair the tall white man quickly turned his knife blade toward the task of taking Dog Kicker's scalp.

Bad Foot was stunned with the speed of what just happened so unexpectedly. He straightened up and stood up right while he tried to get his thinking straight. The white man had great medicine to make the wind blow in his favor. He had to be a great warrior to put three arrows into Dog Kicker so quickly and then come and cut his throat and take his hair.

Bad Foot was the only one to see this. He could tell the story many times over the camp fires of his tribe. He would call the tall white man, Warrior of the Wind.

Dog Kicker was dead. His two wives were now widowed. Doe Skin was no longer a married woman.

Bad Foot flung open the entrance flap and with a broad smile on his thin face he hurried to claim Doe Skin as his new wife.

Jesse turned and started back up the slope toward Woman. Although the wind had died down some, he was now facing into the wind. The dust blew up his nose and into his mouth. To no avail he spat to rid himself of the grit filled saliva. By the time he reached his companion the dust had caused his eyes to turn red and tears formed and ran down his cheeks.

Jesse stopped in front of Woman and angrily thrust the bloody trophy into her hand. "You are the one that wanted it, take it." He wiped his hands on his pant legs and without saying anymore he hurriedly walked by her and mounted his horse.

Woman swung upon her horse and they headed in the direction of the grove of pine trees. When they were even with the trees Woman reined her horse to a stop and turned to face Jesse.

"The Indians will think that you must have big medicine to make the wind blow at your back. They will believe that you are a great warrior to have killed the cruel Dog Kicker and they will give you a name. The name will honor your power as a warrior and they will tell stories about this around the camp fires for a long time. That is the Indian way."

Jesse spat out the words, "It was you that killed him. You're the one that wanted him dead. What makes you think that me, a white man, will be given credit for killing Dog Kicker? Besides I don't want that recognition."

"You were there when Dog Kicker killed Isaac and his warriors charged us up the hill into the wind. One of the warrior's horses refused to run into the wind. The horse shied and jumped sideways and stumbled throwing the rider off. The warrior's arm got tangled in the reins and was drug for a short distance back down the hill. That warrior survived and rode back to safety. He will remember the wind and the dust of that day and know that today the wind was caused by the same great medicine."

"When you were bent over Dog Kicker I saw a small man came out of the tepee across from Dog Kicker's and entered Dog Kicker's tepee. The man that was dragged down the river bank and this one will put their stories together. They will give you a name and it will be repeated around the camp fires."

"I will make a war lance for this scalp to hang from the sharp end of the lance. I will decorate the lance with paint and feathers. Such a thing will bring respect to others and fear to some. Warriors will hesitate before they fight you for you will have a reputation of having powerful medicine."

Bad foot was very happy because both of his wives were happy. This pleased him.

Turtle was happy. With Doe Skin in their lodge Turtle had another woman to help her with her work and guide her in how to do things. This pleased Turtle.

Doe Skin was happy because she had not been beaten nor had Bad Foot even raised his voice since she had been brought to his lodge. This pleased Doe Skin.

Bad Foot mounted Doe Skin as often as he had the energy and time to do so. Doe Skin never objected. Bad Foot and Doe Skin thought she might be with child. This pleased both of them greatly.

In his lodge his life was good and his reputation was also good throughout the men of the tribe. They listened intently to him as he told how the Spirit of the Wind white man took Dog Kicker's life. He had repeated the story many times while sitting around the camp fires at night with the other braves smoking and telling stories.

When urged he would tell the story again and again. "There was a great wind blowing. I was afraid that the lodge would blow away. There was loud shouting outside of my lodge. I looked out the flap to see if I needed to arm myself against an enemy."

"A great and fearful wind was blowing down the hill. It was so strong that sand and dirt and weeds and small branches from trees were carried with the wind. "

"Then by the light of a bright flash of lightening I was able to see the form of a man. I blinked and rubbed my eyes for the man was coming down the hill and the man's feet were not touching the ground. The wind was caring him down the hill. His legs did not move. The wind did not disturb his clothes or his hair. They hung straight down on his body as if there was no wind around him."

"The man of the wind shot three arrows into Dog Kicker so quickly that it was if he pulled the bow string back but once. Dog Kicker was thrown to the ground by the force of the wind and the arrows. When the wind brought the Man of the Wind to Dog Kicker's body it allowed him to drop to the ground, there he knelt to make sure that Dog Kicker was dead and he quickly cut his throat."

"As soon as he had Dog Kicker's hair in his hands he raised both hands up to the sky. It must have been a signal to the gods of the wind for he was then lifted up from the ground again. A bright and strange light shown on him as the wind picked him up and without his feet touching the ground it carried him up the hill."

"The white man was the tall one that joined Isaac and his wife and daughter before the old bearded one was killed by Dog Kicker. He has a powerful medicine and great power to command the wind."

The braves who heard Bad Foot's story were impressed and it made Bad Foot one of them. They smoked together and told their stories but none seemed to match Bad Foot's story.

So it was that among the various Indian Tribes that Jesse Brooks became The Wind Spirit Warrior. He was respected by many and also feared by many.

The storm continued, lightening flashed around them and the wind continued blowing. Woman paid no attention to it and Jesse was forced to follow along after her. Woman and Jesse rode back to their camp in silence. The storm had blown its self out by the time they had reached their camp. They said nothing to one another and bedded down on the ground separated by some distance.

The next morning Woman got up as if nothing had happened and began preparing food to eat. She seemed drawn and distant, but she had been that way ever since her husband and daughter had been killed.

"If we hurry we can move on. We might as well go see the Crows and get rid of these trade goods. There are two rifles to trade; we will get more beaver plews than we can carry."

They met with the Crow Indians and fared well with their trading. When trading the Crow braves would send hidden glances toward Jesse and whisper to one another. It was apparent that they had already heard of Dog Kicker's death.

Woman and Jesse rode home without incident. There were several times that they would catch glimpses of clutches of braves from the distance. However none of them came close they would keep a respectable distance from the one they now knew as the "Wind Spirit Warrior".

By the time they reached the Ponca's settlement winter had settled in. The wind was cold and there were many snow flurries. They arrived home just before a heavy snow began to fall.

They unpacked and stored their possessions away. The white man that was the fur buyer came to their camp and paid Woman in silver coins for the beaver plews. She put the coins in a leather pouch and pulled the draw string shut before nonchalantly dropping it into a corner of the hut.

They occupied the same hut that Woman's family and Jesse had slept in last winter. It did not feel the same. Jesse and Woman made their beds on opposite sides of the hut.

There were many nights that Jesse was awakened by the muffled sobs of Woman. On one such night he got up; picked up his blankets and lay down beside Wind Spirit Woman. Jesse gently touched her shoulder before putting his arm about her. He whispered "Go back to sleep, I am here for you."

To give Woman comfort and support Jesse continued to sleep beside her. They did not sleep together as man and wife. Although they would sleep under the same blankets they did not attempt to consecrate a nonexistent marriage.

One day a Pawnee brave tried showing Woman some attention she pointed at Jesse and lied saying, "I am his wife." None of the braves bothered to approach her again.

It is mid-winter, possibly after Christmas when Jesse began having thoughts about going back to Missouri. Christmas at Uncle Frank's house was always a wonderful time of the year.

His aunt would make candies and sweet cakes and cook a wonderful dinner for all of them. He imagined what it would be like with those six girls squealing with delight and laughing when they opened their presents.

By this time he would be a father. He would have to miss his child's first Christmas. *I wonder if Rebecca had a boy or a girl.*

The thoughts of Rebecca stirred emotions in him, but curiously not the same kind of strong emotions as he once had about her.

Woman and Jesse had been sleeping warm and comfortably together. Woman had been more like her old self lately and rarely did he hear her crying in the stillness of the night.

It was a bright sunny warm winter day. The blue jays darted here and there in the spruce trees as the warmth from the sun melted some of the snow on the southern slopes.

Jesse decided to leave the Pawnee village and go home to see his relatives. He struggled to find the right words. "Wind Spirit Woman, I think that I need to go back to see my family."

Woman lowered her eyes and with her hands gently clasped together she asks, "Is it because of the women, the one that you used to call out her name in your sleep?"

With some hesitation Jesse answered in slowly measured words, "She has a husband and yet is the mother of my child; a child that I have never seen. I don't know if it is a boy or a girl."

He paused; there was a long awkward silence before he continued. "I have an uncle and his family that I want to see. My uncle and his wife have been raising my two sisters."

"There is one other piece of business that I must clear up. When I left, I left in a hurry and I stole Mr. Siegel's white mare. I did leave him a written note that I would pay him for it or return it to him sometime."

"Of course after the mare went lame we traded her off. So I won't be returning her."

Woman shrugged and replied with her simple solution. "You can just steal another horse and give that one to this man."

Jesse laughed, "It ain't that simple. In the Indian world that would be alright. However with the white man's law a man can be hanged for stealing horses."

Later in the day Woman came to Jesse and softly inquires, "If you need to go, when will you leave?"

"It looks like the weather is going to hold and stay warm for a few days. So I reckon tomorrow morning would be as good a time as any."

Woman said nothing as she turned and went into the hut. She returned with the leather bag full of silver coins. "Take these and buy a good horse to replace the one that you took."

"Thank you, but that ain't right that money is yours. The plews that were traded were yours and Isaacs, not mine. You should keep that silver."

She held the bag of coins out to Jesse again. "I can't eat these, when I am hungry they will not fill my belly or keep me warm when I am cold." She insisted, "You take them if they will do you some good."

He hesitated but took the bag of coins. "Thank you, I'll try and find a way to repay you."

"If you leave in the morning what trail will you follow?"

Before he could answer, Kuuruk came and stood quietly and respectfully and would not speak until there was a lull in the conversation.

Jesse looked down at Woman, "The shortest way is going strait south cross country. If I go that way there ain't no real trail to follow but the weather has been good and their ain't much snow on the ground so the going should be easy."

Woman shook her head in disagreement. "It would be safer to go straight to the muddy river and follow it to where your white man's towns are built along its banks. In case there is a blizzard you could hole up with some of the white settlers that live along the river."

111

"Woman, that is good advice but I think I'll go the short way. I just want to strike out on my own. You ain't going to worry about me, are you?"

Woman never answered. Kuuruk spoke up, "Don't worry about Woman while you are gone. I will see that she has food and that no one bothers her."

"I have been the way that you are going. If you want me to I can tell you what rivers that you will come to and where to turn toward the sun to come across the river that is called The Missouri."

"Kuuruk, I thank you for offering to look in on Woman once in a while. If you got time why don't you go ahead and tell me about those rivers."

"You will have to cross some rivers. After you cross the Platte River the first river that you come to will be the Big Blue River. Follow that river south to where it meets with the north fork river of the Big Blue. Ride past this joining of rivers and turn towards the rising sun. In one half days ride you will reach the north fork of the Big Nemaha follow it to the muddy river. From there it will be only a short distance to the place that you seek."

The next morning the fresh snow crunches under foot as Jesse readies his horse for the trip. Some camp dogs rise from their nights slumber to bark at the noise that woke them up.

For the trip Jesse has chosen a long legged well behaved bay gelding. The horses have grown long and shaggy coats of hair to keep them warm during the winter but that doesn't help keep their teeth from aching when they clamp down on an ice cold steel bridle bit. To keep the horses from the discomfort of having a cold steel bit in its mouth he uses a bit less Indian bridle.

Jesse puts the light weight revolver in his winter coat pocket and ties his long bow and arrows onto the back of the saddle. Just before he puts his foot in the stirrup Woman touches him on the shoulder. He turns around and faces her. In the cold air of the morning their breath forms into little puffs of water vapor.

Woman's face is soft and her eyes shiny as she looks up at Jesse. She shyly questions him, "Will you come back here?"

Jess's plan was to go back to Missouri. He had not tried to reason what he would do after that. He did not know how to truthfully answer Woman so he didn't answer her at all.

After an uncomfortable silence Woman hugged him tightly. She held onto Jesse with both arms around his waist she presses her body against him. Suddenly she let go and before he can see the tears in her eyes she hurries back into the hut.

It has been good weather for traveling. The lack of snow has made it easier for Jesse's gelding to have good footing and to be able to find enough dry grass to feed on. For the past few days he has traveled without seeing anyone or having any trouble.

It is rather early in the day and Jesse feels good for he knows the river that he had crossed the previous day was The Big Nemaha River. *It won't be long now. It has been almost two years since I left St. Joe. I am sure that nothing has changed in that time.*

Jesse has been following a well used trail in the edge of a wooded area when in the distance off to his right he got a glimpse of movement. Pulling up on the reins he stops the gelding. In order to get a better look he stood up in the stirrups and looked more closely at the fast moving object.

It appears to be a rider coming quickly across the open prairie to his right. The rider is heading at an angle that is meant to intersect Jesse's course of travel.

Jesse loosens his large buffalo robe cape and reaches for the pistol that is in the belt of his buckskin pants. He stops his horse in time to allow the rider to pass in front of him at a safe distance. The rider turns his horse toward Jesse and slows his horse to a walk as he approaches Jesse. The rider reins to a stop some fifty paces from Jesse.

Jesse could see that the man was well armed. He had a rifle lying across the cantle in front of him and a large pistol in a holster to his right on the outside of his coat. It appears that a double barreled shot gun is strapped cross ways onto the back of the saddle. If that weren't enough weapons there was a gun belt and holster with another big pistol hanging from the saddle horn.

113

The rider held up one hand in a peace sign. "I mean no harm to you. My name's Hood, Daniel Hood." He urged his mount forward toward Jesse at a slow walk and stopped a few feet from where Jesse had reined his horse to a halt.

Mr. Daniel Hood was a small man with a narrow bearded face and quick darting cold blue eyes. He looked tense and ready to take action as if he were afraid someone might jump out from behind a tree and try and shoot him.

Besides being heavily armed the man was dirty and trail worn. His old dirty woolen coat was too large for his narrow shoulders. It was torn in places and patched in others. To hold the coat together he had tied a rope belt loosely around his waist and an old four inch long horse blanket safety pin tried vainly to bring the coat together at his narrow chest. The toes of his boots were worn thin as was his trousers.

Daniel Hood spoke, "I reckon that you know that there are four men behind you. They are pushing their horse fast enough that they will catch up to you shortly."

Jesse was surprised and embarrassed that he did not know that he was being followed. Without thinking he turned and looked over his shoulder. He didn't see any one coming down the trail. But, he couldn't see around the last bend which wasn't that far off in the distance from where he and Mr. Hood were.

Mr. Hood spoke with certainty, "They will be here any minute now. I don't see that you got any weapons to defend yourself with except that bow and them arrows."

He untied the shot gun from the back of his saddle and held it out toward Jesse. Jesse shook his head to reject the offer. "I ain't done nothing to them and I don't know you. I don't have any irons in this fire."

Hood looked toward the bend in the road behind Jesse. "It is too late. Whether you like it or not you're in this fracas."

Hood thrust the weapon toward the reluctant Jesse. "Now take this shot gun. It's loaded with buck shot and some nail heads. If both barrels are fired at a man's gut it will cut him in half. Those men know that so it ain't likely that you'll have to use it." Jesse had been unwittingly entangled in this confrontation. He didn't have a choice so he took the shot gun.

Hood's voice was barely above a whisper as he spat the words out from between his thin lips. "That's Thaddeus T. Tidwell on the left. He is the one I have a quarrel with. You just hold that shot gun on the other three. The weasel faced man in the middle of those three on the black horse is the one you aim that scatter gun at. Don't shoot anyone unless they pull on you."

The four riders reined to a halt a short distance in front of them. Thaddeus T. Tidwell urged his horse forward in front of the others and reined to a stop. None of the riders spoke. There was enough tension in the air that it made the hair stand up on Jesse's arms and the back of his neck.

Out of the corner of his eye Jesse could see Daniel Hood urge his horse ahead a few feet. Mr. Hood seemed relaxed. He held his reins loosely in his right hand and his left hand was inside the front of the oversized faded coat.

Hood looked at the man on the left, "You're Thaddeus T. Tidwell." None of the four men spoke. Mr. Hood leaned forward in the saddle his left hand still on the inside of his coat. He spoke again. He raised his voice slightly, "You're Thaddeus T. Tidwell."

The rider that was directly in front of Hood leaned back in his saddle and answered in a defiant tone. "So what if I am. What business is it of yours?"

Before Tidwell had a chance to say anything else two shots rang out. They were fired so quickly that it sounded like one shot. The force of the two bullets entering Tidwell's chest stood him up in his stirrups. He was suspended there for a couple of brief seconds before he collapsed in a lifeless heap onto the frozen ground.

The sudden loud noise made Jess's mount crow hop to the left but he was able to keep the animal under control. He also managed to keep the shot gun aimed at the other three men.

Although Jesse didn't take his eyes off of the other three men he was aware that Daniel Hood had a smoking pistol in his left hand. Without warning Hood had drawn a hidden pistol from beneath his coat and shot Thaddeus T. Tidwell before any of the four men could draw their weapons.

Daniel Hood turned in the saddle to face the other men. He waved his smoking pistol at them. "I ain't got no quarrel with you men. Ride on while you are still in one piece."

The man on the black horse was the first to turn his mount around. He kicked the horse hard in the ribs. The horse bolted and jumped with all four feet off of the ground. It cut wind as it once again jumped ahead before kicking up clods of frozen dirt as it ran off at a gallop. The other two men weren't long in following.

Hood watched them depart. He then pulled the pistol from the holster that was on his right hip and rode up to the Tidwell's lifeless body. Hood leaned down close to the lifeless Tidwell, held his pistol close to the man's head and blew a large hole in the dead man's forehead. White bone fragments and droplets of blood flew in every direction before they fell onto the snowy ground.

Satisfied, Hood straightened up in the saddle and turned his horse to come up beside the stunned Jesse. Without any show of emotion Hood reached over and took the shot gun out of Jesse's hands and calmly tied it onto the back of his saddle.

Without looking at Jesse, Hood spoke, "Tidwell has a price on his head. He is worth one hundred dollars dead or alive. You can have the reward if you want. Take his horse and gun too. I don't want any of it. I'll help you tie the body onto his horse and you can collect the money from the sheriff in St. Joe."

Stunned with the suddenness and violence of what he had just seen, Jesse said nothing and just shook his head no.

Hood was without any show of emotion as he turned his cold blue eyes in Jesse's direction, "I am going to St. Joe. I would suggest you ride with me. Those three might want to turn around and ambush us, so it's better if we stay together. Do you have a weapon other than that bow and arrows?"

Jesse didn't answer. Hood pulled the gun and holster off of his saddle horn and handed them to Jesse. "Keep these I don't need em.

This pistol is the latest one that was made. It's a .36 caliber Paterson with five rounds, that is a hell of a lot better than a bow and arrows."

Jesse felt like he didn't have a choice but to take the weapons and ride along with Daniel Hood. They came to a hill top some two or three miles from where Tidwell was killed when Jesse turned in the saddle. He could see that the three riders had returned and were dismounted and standing around Tidwell's body.

"I guess that you are right. The three of them have come back and are hovering over Tidwell's body."

Hood didn't turn around, "Like damn vultures picking the bones clean; getting anything off of Tidwell's body that they might put to use."

The two men traveled together without any further conversation. They often turned in their saddles to watch their back trail. They scrutinized every tree and bush that might be a place of an ambush.

Hours later they came to a small creek where there was open water. At that point the creek bed was lined with rocks that keep the water running free of being iced over. Jesse suggested, "Might as well stop and water the horses."

Hood was dismounting as he mumbled, "I'm ready to stretch my legs and relieve myself."

Jesse busied himself loosening the saddle girths and taking the bits out of the mouths of both horses. The horses would be able to drink and take a bite or two of the brown grass that had been exposed by the sun melting the snow along the south bank of the creek.

Hood came and stood silently by Jesse while they waited a while to give the horses a blow. Jesse turned and faced Hood, "I figure that you must be a bounty hunter? Before you shot him you knew that Tidwell had a price on his head, yet you didn't want to collect the bounty. Why is that?"

Daniel Hood didn't answer. Later they swung up into their saddles and rode on. They had ridden for an hour or more before Hood spoke. Hood's horse was to one side and trailing Jesse's horse by a step or two when he began to speak. Jesse was surprised to hear his voice and turned in the saddle to look at Hood.

Daniel Hood spoke in a faraway voice and gazed at the sky as if he were in a dream. "Years ago Thaddeus T. Tidwell was the leader of a bunch of cutthroat killers. Their favorite pastime was to stop at a remote ranch or farm house. When the man of the house showed himself all of them would pull their weapons and fill the poor innocent man full of holes. They would laugh and joke about who shot the man the most times."

Hood continued in a still strangely haunting hollow sounding voice. He continued gazing up at the sky as if he saw pictures in the clouds of what had happened years ago.

"A couple of the men would go kill a cow or calf or some other critter and start butchering it so they could cook it later. The other men would break into the house and violate the wife and any girls that were in the family. They kept this up for three or four days and then some of them would start on a fourteen year old boy."

He stopped talking. Jesse thought that he heard a muffled sob. Then there was a long and dreadfully awkward silence. Jesse turned and looked at Daniel Hood. Hood's skin was pale and his eyes were moist with tears. He was swallowing hard and his hands were trembling as he fought to control himself.

Jesse quickly turned away. He began to imagine what it would be like if that happened to Uncle Frank and his family of seven women. It wasn't a pleasant thing to think about. To get his mind off of that he started to whistle a tune that he had learned as a child.

The sun was sinking leaving a pink glow in the western sky. From somewhere far behind them they heard the yipping of a coyote. It would soon be dark. They crossed the muddy river and rode down the street toward the livery stable. Jesse stopped his horse at the hitching rail outside of the stable.

Hood had reined his horse to a halt in the middle of the street. He shot a brief glance in Jesse's direction and mumbled, "I'm going on ahead." He apparently didn't want any company as he didn't wait for an answer. Daniel Hood, bounty hunter, kicked his tired horse into a trot as he disappeared into the fading light of evening.

After making a couple of loops of the bridle reins around the well-worn hitching post; Jesse entered the stable to look for a stable hand. He neither saw nor heard anyone in the barn and went back outside and stood at the hitching rail. Darkness was falling quickly as it usually does this time of year.

He remembered the last time he came through St. Joe how angry the overweight owner got when Jesse slept in the manger before paying. He stood by his horse and tried to think what he should do.

A voice called out from behind him. "Hello, are you looking to put your horse away for the night?"

Jesse turned and peered into the darkness, the voice sounded faintly familiar. A tall skinny middle aged man appeared out of the darkness.

"You're Sam aren't you?" Jesse said as he peered into the dark.

"Yup, and who am I talking to? Here let me step inside the barn and get a lantern lit."

Sam grabbed a lantern from just inside the barn door and struck a match upon the leg of his trousers and lit the wick of the lantern. He held it up high and stepped closure to get a look at the new customer.

"I remember you. You're the youngster that came through here a year or two ago. You were in a big toot to get out of town. It is good to see you again. You want to put the horse up for a night or two?"

"You have a good memory, yup I want to feed and house my gelding for a day or two. He needs a bit of a rest and so do I."

Sam said with a big grin, "Price ain't gone up any, same as it was two years ago. Are you going to stay here at our stable barn hotel?"

"Sam, I'm just going to board the horse here. I am flush and can pay for a bed. That sounds funny; I ain't slept on a bed for almost two years. By the way where is your over weight and over friendly boss?"

Sam took the reins from the hitching post and led the animal into the barn.

After putting the gelding into a vacant stall and shoveling a generous bucket of oats into the feed trough he coughed and turned to Jesse. "The boss got into an argument."

With a big grin and a laugh Jesse offered, "I can't understand that what with the sweet disposition that he had."

Sam waved his big rough hands, "Well it was a little more than that. The arguing got more and more heated and they started to fight."

"The other man slipped a knife through the Boss's fat belly and it went between his ribs and deep enough inside of his big body to find some vital area. The boss died that night."

"The boss didn't have too many friends. The boss's wife, Bertha, and I were the only two people at his funeral."

"What happen to the guy that stabbed the boss?"

"Since the man that killed the boss didn't weigh more than one hundred and thirty pounds and the boss was twice that big the sheriff let him off saying it was self-defense."

"Sam, that is quite a story. So who's the boss now?"

The light from the lantern fell on Sam's weathered face. Sam pointed toward his chest with a big fore finger. A broad grin lit up his face as he replied, "I am."

Jesse's mouth dropped open. "Well I'll be darned. How did that happen? Sam before you get started; I'm hungry as a bear. Let's go to the café. I'll buy your supper or a cup of coffee or whatever you want and you can finish your story over there."

They were seated at a table when the same overweight waitress wearing the same greasy apron waited impatiently for them to order. She wiped the sweat from her forehead with the apron. In a tired worn out voice she ask, "What do ya want?"

Jesse didn't hesitate, "I'll have some steak and eggs and a cup of coffee. Give the bill to me, please."

Sam ordered a cup of coffee and continued with his story. "Three days after the burial the Mrs. came down to the barn and invited me to come to the house that evening for supper. She said she had to talk to me about the business."

"I didn't know what to think. I was afraid that she was going to fire me or sell the business or something like that."

"That evening after work I washed my hands and face off in the horse's watering tank and trudged up the hill to the old Boss's small house. I wasn't looking forward to meeting with the widow."

"I knocked on the door and the Mrs. answered it and with a sweet smile the Mrs. invited me in. The Mrs. was wearing a nice clean frilly dress. Now mind you she weren't no skinny beauty queen. The Mrs. is kind of overweight, but she has a real nice pretty face with soft brown eyes. She was overweight but she wasn't like the boss. She is just pleasantly plump and she was real nice and polite."

She ask me, "I hope that you like fried chicken and biscuits and gravy?"

"Before I could answer she sat me down at the kitchen table and pulled a corn cob cork from a jug of rhubarb wine. We both had a Mason jar full of that good tasting rhubarb wine before we started eating. That wine sure sat me at ease."

"I caught a whiff of some kind of real nice smelling female toilet water when she was up and serving me my third helping of everything. I thanked her and used her first name, Bertha."

"After I had eaten my fill; the misses told me to call her Bert. Bert said that she wanted me to stay working at the stable and she would double my wages if I would stay."

"She said that she would take care of the money and the keeping of the books and ordering supplies and the like and I could do the stable work. I readily agreed to that."

"Hell, that was easy to agree to. I went back to the stable feeling pretty good. Part of my feeling so good might have been that rhubarb wine."

The next day I was working along and happy as could be with the idea of the Mrs. being my boss when that afternoon she showed up again." She said, "Why don't you come for supper again tonight."

"That night after eating my fill of a delicious stew and another Mason jar full of wine, Bert spoke up."

121

"Sam, I don't like you sleeping down there in that cold barn. You go down and get your belongings and come back and set them in the corner by the door. You can sleep here in the house. It will be warmer and more comfortable than that drafty barn."

"When I came back with my small arm load of belongings I was surprised to see that the Misses had changed into her night gown. She must have put on more fragrance because the room was filled with the scent of her nice smelling toilet water.

"Where do you want me to put these?"

"Sam, you can put them in the bed room."

"I looked around, the house was small and there was only one bedroom. I didn't move."

She smiled sweetly as she took me by the arm, "There is no need for you to sleep on the floor. The bed is big enough for both of us."

"I been sleeping with her ever since. Later on Bert mentioned that she was still young enough to get with child. She wanted to do things proper like. She wanted to be married first in case she happened to get with child."

"So now I am married and one half owner of the stable. She wants to change the name to Sam's Stable and Livery and paint a sign over the top of the front doors. That will have to wait until warm weather."

For the next two days I let my horse have a good rest while I loafed around town. I visited some more with Sam, he seemed so content. Sam being happily married and settled down got me to thinking about such things.

On the morning of the third day I decided to leave. It was a beautiful sunny day. Some pigeons had built their nests in the rafters of the barn. They were cooing and fluttering around among the rafters. I had stepped up into the saddle and was going to ride my gelding out through the barn door when the darn pigeons flew low right by my head on their way outside.

My hat was in my hand. I was afraid that they would release some pigeon poop on me so I quickly jammed my hat down on my head.

The gelding was well rested and so was I. I had pushed the witnessing of Mr. Tidwell's killing and hearing Mr. Hood's story to the back of my mind. It was best if I got as far away from those memories as I could. It was time to enjoy the fine day.

Once I past the town of Conception I began to recognize a few land marks. With some reluctance I was going to have to go past the farm house that the young blonde headed Molly lived in.

I felt guilty and decided to ride out of the way to miss it. It has been almost two years, she probably has gotten married by now, but I still went out of my way to avoid that farm. I guess the best I could do is silently ask her to forgive me for using her to try and forget my own problems.

A couple of days later I reined the gelding to a halt in front of Uncle Frank's farm house. I was surprised that no one came outside to see who it was.

After dismounting I stepped up onto the porch and knocked on the door. A few minutes went by before my sister in law, Sally, opened the door. There was flour on her hands and apron. She held a powdery hand up to shield her eyes and squinted into the direct sunlight that I was silhouetted in.

"Sister in law, it's me, Jesse." It took a few seconds for it to soak in. When it did she stepped past the threshold and grabbed my arm and led me into the kitchen.

"Jesse, what a pleasant surprise, I just started to mix up some bread dough. Sit down here let me get you a drink. Water is all I have. Oh darn, I am so shocked. Let me catch my breath and get my wits about me."

"Take your time Sally. Where's Uncle Frank and the girls too, where are they?"

Sally sat down across the table from me. I took a good look at her as she was wiping her hands off on her apron.

Her hair was messed up as it always was but she didn't look a day older or one pound heavier than when I had left in such a hurry almost two years ago.

Sally said, "Frank is over helping a neighbor with something. Just like him leaving his own work undone to go help someone else. He'll show up for supper. That is for sure."

I was beginning to wonder how much my sisters and my nieces had changed since I had left. I was going to have that answer real soon. There was the sound of several light female voices coming through the open door. They were talking to each other and wondering who owned the horse that had the Indian bow and arrows tied to the saddle.

It sounded as if they had all stopped to give the mount a once over before entering the house. I took that opportunity to step to the door and speak to them.

"Hi ladies, do you like my Indian pony?"

It took them but a second to recognize my voice and look up to see me standing in the door way. All six of them gave out with girlish squeals and pushed one another to try and be the first one to reach me and give me a hug. In the rush to hug me they almost knocked me down. Catching up as many as I could in my arms I returned their hugs.

One young girl stayed back and didn't come charging forward. She was a tall attractive young girl that was more woman than girl. It was my oldest sister.

I spoke to her over the tops of the other five girl's heads, "Mary, my gosh, look at you, why your all grown up."

I took my arms and pushed an opening between two of the girls that were clinging to me and made a path for Mary to come to me. She came forward with measured restraint and with her eyes glistening with tears she shyly slid into my arms and hugged me.

It took a few minutes for everyone to calm down. The girls took turns answering my routine questions as to how old were they now and what grade they were. We went inside and I sat down at the dinner table.

While I held one of the youngest girls on my lap I teased her, "So do you have a boy friend yet?"

There was a silence and five pairs of eyes turned toward Mary. Mary was blushing with embarrassment. Aunt Sally came to her rescue, "Mary has a steady boy friend and they plan on marrying soon, maybe even this spring. He is one of our neighbor's sons and a fine young man."

Once again Sally wiped her hands on her apron. She lovingly hugged Mary's shoulders. "We'll miss her; she is so much help to me and a good big sister to the other girls."

"If you girls will give Jesse room enough to breathe maybe he will tell us what he has been doing for the last two or so years."

I started telling the story of my life of the last two years. I didn't exactly tell everything. For instances I didn't say why I had left and the fact that I stole Mr. Siegel's horse so I could run away. I also left out the parts about the killings. I would probably tell most everything to Uncle Frank but the girls were spared some of the gory details.

Mostly I told the girls about the friends that I had made, Isaac, Wind Spirit Woman, Yellow Flower and Kuuruk, who made the big bow for me. They would ask me questions about where I slept and what we ate and if all the Indians wore war paint and some other silly questions. I tried to answer all of their questions and I stopped only when I heard the sound of Uncle Frank tying up his horse at the hitching rail.

I had been at Franks for two days helping him with his chores and farm work. I finally screwed up my courage enough to ask Frank about my child. No one else was around when I faced Uncle Frank. "Uncle Frank, do you know if Rebecca gave birth to our child?"

"She did."

"Well dang, is that all you got to say?" I don't know why I was annoyed at Uncle Frank. None of this was his doings.

"Have you seen the child? Did she have a boy or a girl? Do you know anything more than just she did?" My temper was coming to the surface. I know that my voice was getting louder and louder.

As always Uncle Frank was calm and unruffled. "The child is a boy. This is Friday the first day of March. Rebecca usually goes to the store for supplies on the first day of the month. She is still living with Shawn but he has never been to the store with her."

"Jesse, you haven't said anything about squaring accounts with Mr. Siegel. I can go with you and we can work something out so I can help you pay for that white mare that you took."

"A boy, well I'll be darned." I took a couple of minutes to mull that over in my mind. "Thanks, Uncle Frank, but I have enough money that I can pay for the mare. I got myself into this mess and I am the one to get myself out of it. I am just hoping that Mr. Siegel isn't going to sick the law on me for stealing."

"Uncle Frank, I'm sorry for getting riled up. None of this has been your fault. I ain't thinking about getting back with Rebecca. She made it clear where she stands and I have thought it through and I know that is the way it should be."

"I do think that I will saddle my horse and ride to the store and see what happens with Mr. Siegel. Hell, facing Mr. Siegel couldn't be any worse than facing a half dozen crazy Indians that wanted to kill me and my friends."

It was a warm and beautiful spring day with the bluebells breaking into bloom beneath the bare branches of the maple and oak trees. Out in the open the bloodroot flowers were beginning to pop up through the soil. There were baby rabbits hopping around in the new grass as I rode up to the store.

Nothing at the store had changed. The porch was still clinging to the front side of the faded board building. I was sure that the porch and the steps needed to be swept clean. I dismounted and went into the darkened interior of the store.

Mr. Siegel was the only person there. He was standing behind the front counter where he kept the cash drawer. I spoke to him, "Hello, Mr. Siegel."

He looked up at me and squinted his myopic eyes from behind thick glasses while trying to figure out what person belonged to that voice.

I thought I would help him identify me. "It's me, Jesse Brookes, Mr. Siegel. I'm the youngster that ran off with your white mare. That was a couple of years ago."

Mr. Siegel had a puzzled expression on his seamed face. He came around the corner of the counter and stood a couple of feet in front of me while he studied my face.

"Oh, my goodness, how you have changed. I didn't recognize you. You're a young man now." He reached up and put a friendly hand on my shoulder and gave it a gentle squeeze.

"Where have you been? No one has heard any news about you for so long; my goodness sake."

I was so relieved, that old Mr. Siegel was truly glad to see me. "Mr. Siegel, I am glad to see you. You look well, I hope that your wife is well too."

"Ya, for our age ve are both well enough. Come on in and set down. Tell me vhat you have been doing."

"Mr. Siegel, I have some old business with you to take care. If you remember I ran away and I took your white mare and an old pistol too. I have brought the pistol back but the mare became lame so I can't bring her back."

Mr. Siegel waved his hand like he was shooing flies away, "Ah, bubkes, I never rode her any way. Besides I haven't had to do the chores and go out and feed and water her. She cost me more in grain and hay than she was worth. I probably should pay you for taking her." He smiled and held his open fingers over his mouth to smother a laugh.

We began visiting. It was if we were old friends catching up on what we had been doing for the past two years. I no longer viewed Mr. Siegel as my employer nor did he look at me as the kid that helped him in the store. It made me feel real good that he treated me as a friend.

To let in some fresh spring air we had left the front door open.. Through the open door I heard the creaking sound of a farm wagon pulling to a stop in front of the store. We interrupted our conversation and waited for the customer to enter the store.

127

A woman with three little children came through the open door way. The woman was carrying the youngest of the three children. It was Rebecca. I took a deep breath and waited for her eyes to adjust to the dim lit interior of the store before I spoke to her.

I was unsure as to what I would say. I stepped forward to where she could see me. I was a bit tongue tied and all I could blurt out was a muffled, "Hello, Rebecca."

She looked up in surprise, studied me for a minute. When she recognized me her eyes widened in surprise. She gasped, "Well, hello, what a surprise to see you here."

It took her only a few seconds to regain her composure and speak sternly to the two older children. "You two can look but don't touch anything."

Still holding the youngest Rebecca turned her attention to me. She held the little one up higher so I could get a good look at him. "This is Will, Will O'Toole, he is a good boy."

Will was a sturdy built tow headed youngster with rosy cheeks and he had Rebecca's green eyes.

Will wanted to get down and had begun to squirm and wiggly in his mother's arms. She put him on the floor and held his hand for a minute. "Now don't go outside and don't touch anything." She admonished, probably to no avail.

Rebecca looked at me rather apologetically, "As you can see Will is very healthy and active too. You can see what kept me busy for the past two years. What have you been doing with yourself?"

I smiled down at her, "Just roaming the country side out west of here. I have been doing some trading and the like."

Both of us were uncomfortable so we just stood there neither one of us really knew what to say. Finally I spoke up, "I am going to go. Mr. Siegel and I had some business matters to clear up. So I guess I'll head back to Uncle Frank's and say good by to him and his family."

Rebecca didn't look at me. "It was good to see you again. Good luck." She turned away from me and chased after one of her errand children as he was climbing onto one of the store shelves to get to something that was out of his reach.

While riding back to Uncle Frank's place I realized how fortune I was. Mr. Siegel wasn't upset with me. I had left thirty dollars with him for the horse and other things that I had taken two years ago. I had gotten to see my son and knew that he was being well cared for.

The only problem that I had was what I was going to do now.

Uncle Frank was in his corn field picking up rocks and putting them on a rock boat. When I yelled at him he stopped and came to the fence. Mopping his brow with his shirt sleeve he gave me his big smile. "I see that Mr. Siegel didn't sick the law on to you."

I replied, "He was real good about everything. I got to see Rebecca, ah Mrs. O'Toole. She had her youngsters with her. The boy is named Will. He is a good looking healthy one. I am glad that he will be raised right because she is such a good mother."

Uncle Frank crossed his arms and rested them atop a fence post and then leaned on them. His mustache twitched a little when he smiled. "What kind of mischief are you going to get into next?"

"I don't rightly know. I like living and roaming around in the open prairie. I know that won't last forever but maybe I'll find something more permanent like after a while. Isaac did it for forty years, but I know that times change and I won't be able to do that for the rest of my life like he did."

"I guess I'll start by going back out to St. Joe and see what happens after that."
I said my good byes to my sisters and other family members and with a sack full of provisions and a clear conscious I turned my gelding toward the west.

When I arrived back in St. Joe I reined up at the stable in hopes that Sam would be there. His familiar voice carried forth from the dark interior of the barn. "Well how about that. I see that they didn't hang the horse thief. Light down and tie your mount up inside here."

I was tying my horse up in a box stall and taking the saddle off and wanting to rub him down when Sam couldn't wait to start talking.

Sam had turned a wooden feed bucket upside down and was sitting on it while he talked. He had a lot to say, telling me about his life with Bertha and how well the business was going and all the various gossip stories of the town.

Sam invited me to come have dinner with him and Bertha that evening at their house. Another home cooked meal sounded real good besides that I had never met Bertha, so I accepted.

After meeting Bertha I realized why Sam spoke of her all of the time. She was a delightful person, easy to talk to and you could see that she really cared for Sam. We visited for an hour before dinner. While Bertha's pie was baking we ate supper. Sam and I were at the table having a second cup of coffee while Bertha got up to take the pie out of the oven.

Sam had a mischievous grin on his face. He leaned over and balanced on one check of his butt. He then let a silent but rancid smelling fart slip out. From where I sat I could smell it.

Bertha had her back to us. She never turned around, "Sam, darn you, I told you not to do that in my house." She scolded him, "You dirty old man, ain't you ever going to learn any manners?"

Sam got up and slipped up behind Bertha. He put his arms around her ample middle and patted her on the stomach. He whispered something into her ear.

I didn't hear a word that he said but I know it pleased Bertha. She giggled like a little school girl and shook her head no before she gently pushed Sam away.

"You sit back down and we'll all have a piece of this fresh apple pie as soon as it cools some."

Bertha sat down next to Sam and directed a question at me. "What are you going to do with yourself now that you have checked on your family?"

It was Sam's turn. "Are going back to that Indian Tribe? You know the one where there was a nice widow woman. It sounded to me like you two got along."

"Yes she is a good woman but I don't know. I did like those people, but as far as she was concerned I believe she is still in mourning over her husband's and her daughter's deaths."

"And then there is another thing, I don't know if I am ready to hook up permanently with someone."

Bertha got up to cut the pie. "Sam, how about Jesse getting a job with that little wagon train that is camped on this side of the river? There scout ran off with their money and left them without an experienced scout."

"That's right, I plum forgot about them. The wagon master has been asking around about some one to help lead them across the plains. I have met the man. He was in the stable looking for some harness repair goods. I think they want to go to the Oregon Territory."

Sam shook his head in disbelief. "They are a bunch of tender foot farmers. I don't know how they made it across the state of Missouri by themselves. They got more junk loaded in them wagons. Why I wouldn't be surprised if the wagons didn't break down before they got very far. The animals could up and die pulling those heavy overloaded wagons."

Sam looked at Jesse. "Jesse, you might be just the right person to show them the way. You know some of the tribes and how to sign."

"I don't know, Sam. Sounds like a big responsibility. Don't know if I'm up to that."

It was Bertha's turn to speak. "It sounds to me like they would be a lot better off with you than without you. If I were you I would go down to the river first thing in the morning and talk to them."

"You know my deceased husband, the boss, he knew one thing. That was how to boss people around and have them get the job done. If you take that job, you tell them farmers that you're the boss and they have to do what you say. Make it clear and stick too your guns."

The next morning before sun rise Sam and I walked down to the rivers edge where the farmers were camped. I was carrying a brand new Springfield model 1842 rifle that had belonged to the boss. Bertha had said that they would never use it and I might as well take it.

131

Some of the farmers were already up and building fires to cook their breakfast mush and heat up their coffee. One farm lady was up and busying herself fixing something to eat.

I noticed that she had two heavy looking boxes tied onto the sides of her wagon. I tipped my hat to her. I wanted to pry and find out some information from her.

"Good morning, my those are heavy looking boxes that you have tied down to the side of your wagon. Do you mind telling me what kind of precious cargo do you have in them?"

She was more than too willing to tell me. She gushed with pride. "Those are filled with my favorite books. I have several bibles and hymnals as well as my favorites. There's Shakespeare and Tolstoy and other great pieces of literature."

She hesitated to catch her breadth, "Can you read?"

"Why, yes ma'am and I can write too." I tried not to show my displeasure in being ask such a question I turned away from her and started walking.

Sam pointed Mr. Baumgartner out to me. He was a big barrel shaped man with a broad back and chest. He had a full beard and a stern no nonsense look on his broad face.

Sam introduced me to Mr. Baumgartner. "Mr. Baumgartner, this here is Jesse Brookes, he is just like you. He is another Missourian. The difference between the two of you is Jesse here has been living among the Indians that are west of here. He knows the country and some of the people. I'm thinking he might be able to help you and your group out."

I was wearing my moccasins and buckskin britches. Mr. Baumgartner looked me over like I was a farm animal that he was considering buying. I waited for him to speak.

After his careful inspection Mr. Baumgartner cleared his throat, "We are concerned about the heathens. We have done considerable praying about having safe passage but it would be comforting to have someone with us that was familiar with those red skinned uncivilized people."

"We are God fearing peaceable Christians and wouldn't know the first thing about how to fight them off during an attack."

That kind of talk put Jesse back on his heals. He stared at the big German for several minutes while he gathered his thoughts before speaking.

"Mr. Baumgartner, in all due respect, being attacked by Indians isn't your biggest danger." Jesse hesitated long enough to let his words soak in.

Mr. Baumgartner was startled. With a rush of exhaled air from his big chest he exclaimed. "Well if that ain't the most dangerous thing out on that vast prairie; what is?"

"Being unprepared for the long journey. That means taking possessions that will weigh down your wagons and wear out your work animals. When your wagon train starts into the higher country those animals will be pulling uphill for weeks. By the time this train reaches Fort Laramie they will be played out. Some of the animals might even die before they get that far."

"After that they will have to pull those loads over some very unfriendly rugged mountains. The mountains are the likes of which you ain't never seen before."

Baumgartner was obviously perturbed by this unexpected advice. He stammered as he spoke with spittle flying from his fat lips, "Why all of these work animals are in the finest of condition. I don't believe that it would be any problem for them."

Without flinching Jesse looked directly into the eyes of the big German. "I just got through telling you that being unprepared is going to be your worst enemy. If I am going to be your guide or scout or whatever you want to call me you have to believe what I tell you and do as I say. You don't seem willing to do that."

Jesse hesitated for a few seconds before he turned and started to walk away.

Mr. Baumgartner waited until Jesse and Sam were quite a distance from him before he called him back. "Wait, wait a minute, don't be in a haste to go." Baumgartner reached out his hand to stop

133

Jesse. "I don't quite understand what it is that we must do to be prepared for this journey."

Jesse stopped and walked back to face Baumgartner again. He decided to heed Bert's advice about being a boss. "The very first thing for you to agree to is I am in command. I am the boss. I will tell you what these folks are to do and you make them do it. To your people you will appear to be the boss. Do you understand that?"

Baumgartner swallowed hard before asking in a defeated tone, "I Still don't know what you want us to do to be prepared."

"You and I will go through every single wagon. To lighten their loads we will have the owner unload and leave the unnecessary things here. We will start with your wagon. That will show the others that you are sincere."

Jesse continued, "The travelers will take only food, water, blankets and clothes. No frilly fancy clothes, just the ones that are serviceable on the trail. They will need medicine, laudanum if they have it and surgical tools. Weapons and cook gear, those are the things that are necessary to survive. When do you want to start?"

"Oh, one other thing I will be with you only as far as Fort Laramie. Do you agree?"

In a low subdued voice the usually blustery old German agreed. "Can we start right away?"

"We will start as soon as I get my horse and gear and say good bye to my friends." Jesse and Sam turned their backs on Mr. Baumgartner and walked hurriedly toward the stable.

While they were walking Sam spoke up, "I think you did a right good job of that, Mr. Boss-man."

Back at the stable Jesse was going through his saddle bags when he found something that Woman had hidden there. She had tightly wrapped the two Indian scalps in a piece of leather and bound them tightly with a raw hide throng.

I suppose that superstitious woman thinks these will be strong medicine and bring me good luck. He rewrapped them and stuck them back into the saddle bags.

He felt well-armed with the pistol that Hood had given him and the Boss's rifle along with his long bow and arrows.

Jesse rode back to the wagon train where he saw Baumgartner and a stout woman standing beside a wagon. The news must have gotten around about lightening the loads for there were a dozen men and women idly standing nearby.

He dismounted, "Is this yours?" He pointed toward the wagon.

Glumly Mr. Baumgartner nodded his head yes. His wife's face was solemn as Jesse climbed into their wagon. Jesse called out to them. "This big oak chest that is full of dishes must go."

Dutifully Mr. Baumgartner helped Jesse unload the heavy chest. The Mrs. had tears in her eyes as they sat it on the ground. She spoke, "It was my grandparents set of good china." She was unable to think about her lose and she turned and walked away.

Jesse and Mr. Baumgartner went through each wagon and unloaded what Jesse deemed as unnecessary weight. They unloaded heavy farm plows, cook stoves, and many other items that weren't deemed necessary for the journey. No one voiced an objection although it was clear that they didn't appreciate what their new scout was doing.

The farmers unloaded books, oak furniture, plows and wedding dresses etc. Some of the women cried as they set their belongings down in the dust to allow strangers to come get it or have it fade and fall apart in the sun and rain. Baumgartner was forceful but with a gentle hand and recited biblical passages as they worked The women didn't like Jesse for making them throw away items that they felt were important.

No one spoke an objection until they came to the last wagon to be emptied. It was the wagon that had the two boxes of books tied to it.

The woman stood in front of one of the wooden boxes of books with her arms folded over her chest and her chin stuck out defiantly. "Adolph Baumgartner, don't you dare touch my precious books. Many of them are works of the Lord."

Bewildered, Mr. Baumgartner stopped directly in front of the lady and in an apologetic tone, "Rachel, I am sorry but everyone else has done what they need to do to lighten their wagons. I would be pleased if you would submit to our request."

While Rachel stepped forward and stuck her face up close to Mr. Baumgartner, Jesse slipped around her, pulled out his sharp skinning knife and cut the ropes holding the box onto the side of the wagon. The box was so heavy with books that it burst open as it hit the partially frozen ground. Jesse quickly stooped down and picked up a thick leather bound book.

Rachel's face twisted in rage, "Heathen, may the wrath of the Lord strike you down for such insolence."

Jesse held the book up and shook it at Rachel. "This is some of Shakespeare's works, about Oedipus and Hamlet. He writes about murder, and suicide. Then there is the occult, ghosts and even incest in his writing."

He mocked her, "I think it would only be right for a pious woman like your self to be rid of such ungodly trash as this." He used the toe of his moccasin and kicked some of the books into the dust away from the broken box.

"Mr. Baumgartner, if you would be so kind as to break the other box open while I climb into the wagon. Mr. Baumgartner, don't you think it only right to allow this God fearing lady to keep two bibles, two hymnals and two works of literature?"

Rachel didn't try to stop them. She stood perfectly still her face red and her neck bulging with pent up anger and frustration.

By now most of the people of the wagon train had assembled and had watched the removal of Rachel's books. Rachel's husband, Henry, was among the onlookers.

Jesse decided that it was time to speak to them. "Mr. Adolph Baumgartner has told you that I will guide you across the prairie. I didn't enjoy doing this no more than you liked me throwing your things away. It is a long difficult trip and I intend to do everything that is necessary to get everyone of you there safely. We will begin crossing the river at noon."

Jesse relied on Adolph's experience to get the wagons across the wide but shallow Missouri River. It pleased the old German to be included in the decision making and for Jesse to defer to his experience. In the following days they became close friends and worked well together while directing the people of the wagon train.

After a few days on the trail Mr. and Mrs. Baumgartner invited Jesse to have an evening meal with them. Their oldest daughter, Heidi, helped prepare and serve the meal.

Heidi was an attractive blue eyed buxom blond girl in her mid-teens. She kept sneaking approving looks at Jesse when she thought no one was looking. Jesse chose to ignore her as if he didn't know that she was interested in him.

They had finished their dinner of potatoes and sausages and some German black bread when they sat down to relax. Mr. Baumgartner was sitting on the wagon tongue and Jesse sat on the ground with his legs folded beneath him.

Mr. Baumgartner burped and then cleared his throat as if he was preparing to give a lengthy speech. "That Rachel woman is going to hold a grudge against you until she dies. She doesn't think much of me either. I would like to ask you a personal question. I hope that I don't offend you."

"You feel free to ask me anything that you want to. By the way, do you mind if I call you by your first name. Calling you Mr. Baumgartner seems awful formal for my taste."

"I would be pleased if you addressed me by my first name. After all it may make this long trip seem a little shorter. When we were unloading Rachel's books you stopped her objections cold when you knew what those fancy books were about. How did you know about them?"

Jesse had a pleased look on his face and a slight smile played at the corners of his mouth. "Let me tell you about my folks. When I was about fourteen my folks were killed by lightening. They were in a wagon riding home from church when they were struck by a bolt of lightening. That made me and my two younger sisters orphans."

"I still have a hard time figuring out why two people who had been attending church were killed by an act of nature. Especially since nature is supposed to be controlled by God."

Mr. Baumgartner offered, "God gives and takes away. We seldom understand why. Please go on."

"I was educated by my mother. That is why I knew of those authors. Mom was a teacher and she loved the finer things, like literature and music. Boy, did she make us read some boring books. At least at the time I thought it was punishment to sit still during the cold winter nights and read those thick books. Shakespeare was one of the authors that we had to read. "

"Mom played a violin that her dad had given her and she played the piano too. The only piano in town was at the local saloon. She had a beautiful voice and could sing like a bird. I can see my mom now. She was tall and slender and very attractive. My oldest sister looks just like our mother."

"One Saturday afternoon our family was in town getting our monthly provisions when we heard piano music coming through the open door of the saloon. The music was badly off key but mom started humming with it any way. All at once she stopped walking and looked toward the open door of the saloon."

"Dad said, no, no, I know what your thinking, now please get in the wagon and lets head on home."

"Mom just smiled and threw her shoulders back and marched right in through that open door. The four of us were shocked and dumb founded we just stood in the street as if our feet had taken roots in the dirt."

"In just a few seconds the piano music became pretty as could be. It wasn't long until mom began singing in her beautiful clear voice. After a while some other women joined in. Dad just shook his head. We went over by the saloon and sat down in the shade on the board walk to wait for mom."

"After about an hour of being serenaded the music stopped. We could hear the excited voices of several women and then mom appeared at the open door way. She turned and waved goodbye to some people that remained inside of the darkened saloon."

"With a big contented smile on her face she said she was ready to go home now."

There was a long silence as Jesse continued thinking about his family. Mr. Baumgartner was silent. He knew it was best to let Jesse be the one to break the silence.

"So, that is the story of my childhood. I am sorry if I got carried away about my Mom."

The weeks went by as the wagon train crept slowly through the plains toward Fort Laramie. Once the wagons were on the move in the early morning, Jesse would ride ahead and scout the trail for water and hazards and hopefully kill a deer or other game for fresh meat.

He and the men of the wagon train got along but most of the women still held a grudge against Jesse for him dumping their belongings out to be left behind. Rachel spoke out vehemently against Jesse every time that she had someone that would listen to her.

The wagon train was following the Oregon Trail for big wheel wagons that ran on the south side of the Platte River. Jesse was riding his gelding beside the lead wagon when he reined his horse to a halt. He turned in the saddle and motioned for the wagon train to keep moving while he sat on his horse and gazed down a steep river bank toward the river.

This is the place; the place where Isaac and Yellow Flower died. The tree we took refuge behind is still there. Oh, how it hurts to think of the two of you dying like that. I wonder where Spirit Woman is right now. She seemed sad when I left.

A voice from the trail broke into his thoughts. "Are you all right?" It was Mr. Baumgartner calling out to Jesse.

Jesse never answered. He just raised a hand and waved and then urged his horse forward to the front of the lead wagon.

That night after their animals were cared for and everyone had eaten their supper Jesse approached Mr. Baumgartner. "Adolph, the trail is going to get rougher for the wagon teams. We will start to going up hill every day. In another two or three weeks we'll reach

139

Chimney rock. That is in the edge of the Big Horn Mountains. The air will be thinner and the trail will be more difficult."

"I have noticed that the grazing isn't as good now. There has been a large herd of animals with the wagon train that is ahead of us. Their herds have been eating the grass down pretty badly. Also the grass in this higher country is tougher and isn't as nourishing as the grass that your animals are used to. You are going to have to keep watch on the animals and see that they are well cared for."

"We are getting into Sioux Indian Country. Tell your people to be on the look out and for God's sake don't let any of the kids or women folk stray out away from the wagons even in broad daylight."

"Keep the children and young women close by. The Indians like to steal little children and young women. They can swoop in and grab someone and be gone before any one realizes it."

It was getting mid summer, the days were hot and dry. The wind blew relentlessly day in and day out. The days were long and tiring on the men and their families as they trudged slowly threw each hot dry dust filled day. They breathed in the dust, spit out dust and ate dust with almost every bite during meal time. Sun burned and foot sore they kept moving toward their destination.

Jesse tried to be encouraging by telling them it wouldn't be long before they would see Chimney Rock. Reaching Chimney Rock was their short term goal. This morning was like every other one for the past month. Before leaving to scout for the night time camp site he would confer with Mr. Baumgartner about the welfare of the people, animals and wagons of the wagon train.

This morning was like all the rest. Jesse saddled his gelding and rode off to scout for a good place to make the evening camp. He kicked the gelding into a trot stirring up a cloud of dust as he rode ahead in search of grazing and water for the camp site.

On his return he was wiping his sweaty forehead with his shirtsleeve when he rode to the top of a gentle rise. From there he could see the wagon train. Something was wrong. There wasn't any trail dust being kicked up by the plodding animals. The wagons weren't moving.

Pulling on the reins he stopped his horse and stood up in the stirrups to get a better look. There were three men who appeared to be confronting a group of people from the wagon train. The three men had their backs to the river and it appeared that they had someone tied to the spokes of one of the lead wagons. One of the strangers was holding the pilgrims at bay with a long rifle.

Jesse squinted his eyes and held his hand over them to shield out the sun. "Damn, that's the three men that were with Tidwell." He cursed out loud to himself.

The river bank was low and sloped gently toward the water. It wouldn't afford him much cover to come up behind the men. But, that was his only chance to surprise them while they were occupied with bedeviling the settlers.

Jesse checked his pistol and then eased his mount over the bank. When they got within several yards of the outlaws he dismounted, and tied his horse to a small willow tree. To avoid being seen he ran stooped over to where he was directly below the three men.

Jesse got down on his stomach and crawled to the top of the river bank. To get a good look he took his hat off used his hands to part some slew grass. He was only a few yards away from the three men. Two men had their backs to him and stood facing Rachel. The third man was holding the crowd of settlers at bay with a rifle.

They had tied poor Henry up to the spokes of a wagon. His back was to the wagon and his arms spread out as if he was to be crucified. The little man who was barely an inch or two over five feet tall had been stripped of his shirt. He was as bony and thin as his wife Rachel was full bodied and muscular.

The two men who had their backs to Jesse were busy tormenting Rachel. The left side of her face was bloodied and bruised. There was no doubt that she had not given in without a fight or at least giving them a piece of her mind. Blood dripped from a wound on her left check onto her torn blouse. The dripping blood added to the large bloody area that was on her blouse.

They may have hit her but they didn't knock the fight out of her. Rachel's eyes blazed with resistance and her teeth were clenched and her jaw was set as she starred defiantly at the two men in front of her. If looks could kill they would have been dead.

Jesse hoped that she or Henry wouldn't give him away to the outlaws as he rose up from the bank and prepared to run forward and stick his pistol into the ribs of one of the killers.

Jesse stood up and cocked his Paterson pistol as he ran quickly across the short distance toward the two outlaws. He made sure that he could have a clear view of the one man that already had a weapon in his hands. He yelled out, "Drop your weapon or I'll shoot you. Don't even turn around." Jesse stopped and raised his pistol with both hands fixing his sights on the man with the rifle.

The man with the rifle turned to see who was challenging him. He began to raise his rifle. Jesse didn't give him a chance to bring the sights of the rifle on him. He fired immediately and saw the renegade drop his rifle and fall to the ground grasping at his left leg.

The other two had been so completely surprised that they failed to even draw their pistols before Jesse turned on them. "Go ahead," He challenged. "I got enough powder left to blow you both to hell."

One of the men looked over at the other one and slowly elevated his hands. After some thought the remaining man did likewise. Jesse recognized the last man to raise his hands as the weasel faced man that was the middle man on the black horse when they met Tidwell. His cold gray eyes widened as he recognized Jesse.

Jesse felt the tension between the two of them and moved his pistol slightly so that it was aimed directly at that man's chest.

Jesse yelled out commands, "Adolph, get someone over here to unarm these two and pick up that rifle from the one I shot. Quickly, damn it be quick about it. Someone come and cut poor Henry down."

Rachel had already moved over to where Henry was tied to the wagon wheel. Her hair was messed up and her face bloodied but without hesitating she went to aid her husband. She was trying without success to untie the ropes that bound him to the wagon wheel.

After Adolph had disarmed the men Jesse gave them orders. "You two men move over there by your wounded partner."

"Adolph get someone to gather up all of their firearms, the ones on their horses too and throw them in the river. While you're at it you better check their boots and under their shirts to see if they have any small weapons hidden on them. Throw all of the guns in the river."

Jesse continued, "Now you three; get on your horses and get out of the range of my Hawkins Rifle. I will not hesitate to shoot you if you come within range of my rifle."

The two men hurriedly helped the wounded man up on his horse and held on to him as they rode back along the river to the east of the wagon train. Jesse saw them stop about one half mile away. They dismounted and helped the wounded man from his mount and laid him down on the ground.

Jesse was standing still watching the retreat of the renegades when Henry and Rachel came up behind him. Rachel was holding a wet towel to her swollen and bloody face. She tossed her modesty aside and ignored her torn blouse.

Henry was buttoning his shirt over his thin chest and spitting on his hand to smooth down his thinning hair. He was the first to speak to Jesse

"It didn't look good for either one of us. We are grateful that you came to our rescue." He offered his hand and with a surprisingly strong grip shook Jesse's hand. For the first time since they had met Rachel looked at Jesse without being angry at him. It was the only time since they had met that she didn't have that hateful look in her eyes.

Her thank you sounded unlike any voice that Jesse had heard coming from her.. Rachel spoke in a soft feminine gentle tone. "I too am grateful to you, thank you."

Jesse acknowledged their gratefulness, "I did what I had to." Somewhat embarrassed he made an abrupt retreat to retrieve his horse. He reloaded his pistol and stood at the bank of the Platte River keeping an eye on the three men that had dismounted and were attempting to tend to their wounded comrade.

He was so intent upon watching the three men that he didn't hear Adolph, Rachel and Henry approach him from the rear.

Adolph spoke first, "Jesse, we have decided to go help the wounded man. Before you say anything I want to tell you why."

"We feel like it is our Christian duty to help him. As Christians we are supposed to help all people that are hurting, friend or foe."

"What the," stammered Jesse. "Those damn men were thinking about killing Henry and who knows what they would have done to Rachel. And there you God fearing people stood and watched. You didn't lift a finger to help two of your own."

"Now you want to risk your necks to tend to that injured galoot."

Before he could continue Rachel interrupted Jesse. "I know that it is hard for you to understand. You see it is our belief to turn the other cheek. In other words if an enemy strikes you we will not fight back but show them the love of God. Our belief is to not do battle nor fight with other human beings."

With his jaw clinched tightly Jesse murmured, "I'll get my rifle and come along."

Adolph vetoed that, "No we must go unarmed. That will show our good will. Since you were the one that shot the man, it would be best if you remained here. I hope that you would try to understand our way."

Exasperated; Jesse looked down at his feet and held both hands up shoulder high and shook his head and hands in resignation to their desires. "Go, do whatever it is that you think is right. Just don't expect me to come to your rescue again."

The three marched resolutely forward using a piece of old white clothe tied to a how handle for their truce flag. Rachel was caring a black medicine bag while Henry held the flag aloft. Adolph carried a gallon jug of clean water and some rags for bandages.

The three medical missionaries came to a halt in front of the two men that were standing waiting and watching their approach. The injured man lay on his back on the dry bunch grass. Nothing had been done to care for his wound.

Adolph sat the jug on the ground as if they meant to be there for some time. "We are Christian people who feel it is our purpose to help the sick and injured. We are here to care for the man with the pistol ball in his leg. We are not here to quarrel with you."

"Henry stepped forward and in a loud clear voice spoke directly to the two uninjured men. "My wife has helped many injured people. She is very capable person when it comes to setting broken bones, mending cuts and gun shot wounds. That is why she has a bag full of the right tools to help this injured man."

Before he had finished Rachel had already moved toward the injured man. "What is his first name?"

"The small sharp faced man with the cold eyes showed no emotion and said nothing. The other man stepped forward, "It is Will, he is my older brother. I hope that you can help him. If nothing is done that wound will get infected and he will die."

Rachel began by calling the man by his name in a soft reassuring tone and telling him that they were there to care for him and not to worry that he would survive.

The trio of good Samaritans busied themselves cutting away the man's pant leg and cleaning the wound with water from the jug.

While Adolph, Henry and Will's brother held Will down Rachel probed for the musket ball. It didn't take long before she brought the ball out of the man's bloody torn flesh using her small shiny forceps. Triumphantly she held it up for all to see as she squealed with delight.

After cleaning and bandaging the wound she instructed the brother to remove the bandage twice a day and clean the wound and put on a fresh bandage. She then washed her bloody hands with the remaining clean water.

While Rachel was putting her instruments away Adolph spoke. "Let's pray." He said a brief prayer and unharmed the three good Samaritans walked back to the wagon train.

Days later the wagon train was approaching a tributary of the Wind River when Jesse stopped his horse and stared into the distance. *This is where Isaac and his family and I met some Crow Indians for trading. I suppose Spirit Woman is still in mourning. On the other hand I doubt that a woman ever forgets the death of a child. Maybe someday she can be able to go on with her life.*

It was his habit to swing out in a wide arch on the way back to the wagon train. He kept his eyes on the ground in search of tracks that might reveal the presents of strangers. Seeing something suspicious he dismounted to look more closely at what appeared to be the tracks of some unshod horses.

The first thing that Jesse did when he returned to the wagon train was find Mr. Baumgartner. "Adolph, I ran across some fresh tracks. It looks like there are five or six Indians that have been hiding in the rocks and keeping track of us. It is for sure that they are Indian ponies. One of the ponies leaves a really big hoof print."

"By the sign that I saw it is my guess that we have been watched for at least two days. They have been staying out of sight and just keeping pace with us."

Adolph's eyes opened wide with surprise. He stammered, "What do you think they want?"

"It's a small party of warriors. They won't be looking to come at us directly. They are probably looking to steal some horses or maybe some children. They might just be curious about us and what we are doing out here. To be safe you tell your people to be sure and not go out in the brush for any reason."

"Adolph, there is one other thing; I know that your people don't fight but you better be damn ready to if they come after one of us."

On the hill side above the wagon train five Dakota Sioux warriors sat impatiently waiting for orders from their leader, Spotted

Horse. They sat behind some scattered boulders out of view of the pilgrims in the wagon train.

The leader was a large broad shouldered man. His massive body and well muscled arms had many scars on them from the many battles that he had been in. He was known and feared by the many tribes of the area for his bravery and ruthlessness.

He was mounted on an Appaloosa Indian pony. He always rode the large spotted horse into battle. His horse was a huge black stallion with white hind quarters that were covered with black spots. The stallion was easy to track for it left huge deep hoof prints in the trail.

Long before he had his black and white spotted horse the big brave had seen a spotted horse like the one he rode and he desired it but the horse that he saw was too old. He was told there were a people that had large herds of such animals. They were the Nez Perce Tribe that lived in the far away mountains of the northwest.

The big warrior was determined to have such a horse. He traveled for two moons to reach the Nez Perce's territory. Soon after arriving there he saw a large herd of spotted horses. He remained hidden during the day time while watching the herd.

He saw a large well muscled black stallion with black spots in a white blanket on its rump. That was the one he wanted for his own. He would wait until night fall to steal the stallion from the Nez Perce.

He then picked out an old mare that had trouble grazing because her teeth were worn down short. The big brave pulled many handfuls of fresh tender sweet grass. To mask his scent he covered himself with fresh horse droppings. Once it was dark he moved slowly and quietly among the herd of horses until he came to the old mare.

Rubbing her neck and speaking softly to her he fed her the grass. Once they were friends he nudged her until they stood beside the stallion. The big brave worked patiently and gently with the stallion until he was able to slip a rawhide noose around its neck and lead it away from the herd.

During the next several seasons the big brave rode the Appaloosa in many battles. While fighting bravely and fiercely he received many wounds that left scars on his chest and arms. He was easily recognized for his spotted horse and his large scarred body. He was called Spotted Horse.

One of the younger more impatient braves spoke to Spotted Horse. "We have watched for two days. Let us steal some horses or do something. These people are foolish they do not even carry their rifles."

Another warrior spoke. "Do you not have eyes? They don't have any horses worth stealing. The scout is the only one with a good enough horse to steal. I have trailed him. He rides an Indian pony. I know that is an Indian pony because it is without the irons that white men put on their horses hooves."

The warrior went on, "The scout wears moccasins but looks like a white man yet he carries a long bow on his saddle."

The impatient brave spoke again, "Maybe he is a half breed. There are six of us. Why would we need to worry about one scout?"

Spotted Horse spoke, "These people are poor. They have nothing useful."

A third brave spoke, "There is a white haired young girl that leaves the wagons each morning. She is by herself and goes into the brush to pass water. She has done so for the past two mornings."

With that news Spotted Horse looked pleased. "We shall take her early tomorrow morning while she squats down in the brush." He put his right hand on his crotch and rubbed it for a while. "I feel the need for a woman."

Early the next morning two Indian braves leapt from their hiding place in the bushes and carried Heidi away. Before they had grabbed her she had pulled her underclothes down around her ankles. During the brief struggle her under garment came off and was caught in the top of some bushes.

Mr. Baumgartner was up and ready for Heidi to help his wife fix breakfast. He became upset that his daughter was no where in sight. He demanded of his wife. "Where is that girl?"

In a calm soothing voice Mrs. Baumgartner replied. "She is probably up there on the hillside doing her morning toiletries." She pointed toward the hillside as she spoke.

Mr. Baumgartner was not pacified, "She knows that she isn't supposed to leave the wagons. Why would you let her do such a foolish thing?"

"Adolph, calm down. You know how sensitive young girls are about such things."

After she finished chastising her husband Mrs. Baumgartner looked toward the hill side and saw Heidi's underclothes clinging to the bushes.

She tugged at Adolph's sleeve and pointed at the hillside. "Adolph, some things wrong!!!"

Mr. Baumgartner bellowed at the top of his lungs for Jesse. He told Jesse that Heidi was missing and pointed to the underclothes that were caught on the bushes and flapping in the breeze.

Without saying a word Jesse turned and ran for his horse. After hurriedly saddling the animal he tied his bow and arrows on the back of the saddle, grabbed his Springfield rifle and Paterson pistol and sprang into the saddle.

"Stay here" he commanded "they couldn't have more than one half hour head start." He kicked his horse in the ribs and galloped to the top of the ridge where he saw the marks in the rocks where the horses had been.

Their trail will be difficult to follow in these rocks. It is going to be hard to catch them. They know where they are going and I don't. I can't waste time if I am going to try and save that stupid girl from harm.

He kept his mount moving at as fast a pace as he could and still be able to follow the horse's tracks scratched in the rocky soil. He looked up from time to time to see if any of the Indians were checking on their back trail.

The tracks led him out of the rocks and down into a small valley where the soil gave better evidence of the pace of the horses that he was following. By studying the tracks it appeared that they weren't in any hurry.

It was still morning as Jesse's chase led him into some more rocky country. The wind was blowing harder as he entered an area that had many small canyons and eroded gullies.

The tracks were heading toward one of the small canyons. Jesse reined his horse to a halt. *It's* time *to look things over; no need to run into an ambush. The trail appears to be going into that box canyon. They may have posted a lookout at the mouth of the canyon. The left canyon wall is the tallest. That would be the most likely place to have a lookout.*

Circling around to his left he stayed above the rim of the canyon. "There he is!!" A young warrior was standing nonchalantly shifting his attention from the back trail to the back of the dead end canyon. He seemed much more interested in what was going on at the end of the blind canyon than watching the back trail.

Quietly dismounting Jesse untied his bow and slipped up behind the unsuspecting young brave. He was hoping to get close enough to be able to put an arrow into the brave's neck. If he was fortunate the shot through the brave's throat would keep him from making any loud noises that would alert the others of his presence.

Stopping some forty feet away Jesse pulled the bow string taut and released the arrow. The brave quivered, and clutched at the arrow in his throat and with a muted gurgling noise coming from his pierced wind pipe he dropped to the ground.

Picking up a large rock Jesse rushed forward and struck the young brave in the head with it. He took a quick look at the fallen man, threw the bloody rock down and ran quickly to get in his saddle. He rode down the steep slope onto the floor of the canyon.

When he reached the canyon floor he saw that the entrance to the dead end was narrow. A short distance into the canyon was a curve in the walls. The offset wall kept Jesse from seeing the end of the canyon. If he kept to the right side they wouldn't be able to see him coming until he got to the curve in the wall.

He cautiously walked the gelding along the wall. Dismounting he peered around the corner. Fifty paces away was the entrance where the canyon ended in a large hollowed out room.

Another guard was posted at the entrance. He too wasn't taking his job seriously he looked like he was dozing. He was squatted on his haunches. To keep the barrel of his rifle out of the dirt he laid his rifle upon a small rock. He had pulled a torn faded clothe up over his head and neck to keep the wind and dust out of his eyes.

Jesse checked his pistol and made sure all five chambers were loaded with ball and powder. He stepped into the saddle, with strung bow in his hands he took a deep breath and guided the gelding out onto the canyon trail. The sentry didn't look up.

The sentry woke up when Jesse had ridden within a few yards of him. The groggy guard reached for his weapon as he struggled to his feet. Jesse's arrow penetrated deep into the Indian's chest. Grabbing at the arrow with both hands he dropped to his knees. For a brief time he struggled with the arrow before falling face first into the rocky soil.

Jesse quickly dropped his bow and pulled his rifle from the saddle scabbard. With a war cry he kicked the gelding into a charging gallop and rode through the opening of the dead end canyon.

Their Indian ponies were hobbled and tethered to some scrub brush on the right side of the canyon wall. Two men were kneeling over a stone fire ring in the center of the hollowed out room.

Toward the back of the room the half-naked Heidi was being held down by one warrior. There was a huge ugly broad shouldered brave standing at her feet. He had dropped his leggings down. He was struggling to kick free of his clothing that was tangled around his ankles.

Jesse's horse plunged through the opening into the big room. He raised his rifle and shot the first man that got to his feet that was working at the fire ring. Jesse's horse leaped over the low rocks of the fire ring making the other warrior dodge to one side to keep from being run over by the horse.

Jesse then had time to grab his rifle barrel in both hands and swing it as hard as he could at the man's head. His aim was good, but the rifle stock wasn't up to the punishment. It broke in half and fell to the ground along with the bludgeoned warrior.

He dropped the broken rifle and leaped from his horse. Landing on his feet he fought to gain his balance. Once he had his balance he pulled his pistol from his holster and fired two shots at the man holding Heidi to the ground. The first shot hit him in the shoulder making him spin around. The second .36 caliber ball caught him squarely in the middle of the chest. He toppled over backwards and lay still.

Heidi was screaming, Jesse's spooked horse ran out the entrance of the big room. The Indian ponies were pulling at their tether and jumping around trying to get free to run from the noise and confusion.

The big broad shouldered warrior had finally freed his feet from the tangled clothes. He was naked from the waist down. There was a knife in his hand. He let out a bone chilling scream and gathered himself as he was about to charge down the slight incline and attack Jesse.

Jesse cocked his pistol again and fired. The ball struck the scarred shoulder of the warrior. It didn't faze him as he came off of the ledge with a leap and landed directly in front of Jesse.

Jesse cocked and fired his pistol twice more as quickly as he could. He saw blood and bits of flesh fly as one ball hit the warrior in his scarred chest. Even that direct hit didn't slow him, but the last ball struck the big Indians stomach. Blood from his stomach spurted forward and splattered on Jesse's shirt.

To avoid the man's charge Jesse jumped backwards. An expression of surprised shock came over the huge man as he lost the use of his legs and fell at Jesse's feet. His legs were no longer at his command. They were useless to him. The ball that had entered his stomach had passed on through and severed the spinal cord in his back. It caused him to lose all use of his body from the waist down.

Jesse realized the big ugly scarred warrior's legs were useless. He backed up more so he could not be reached and reloaded the five chambers of his pistol.

The big warrior's face was contorted in rage, his eyes bulged as he screamed at Jesse. With his knife still in his hand he tried to pull his useless lower body forward using only his powerful arms. He knew he was going to die and it made him manically intent on taking Jesse's life before he died.

For a brief second Jesse saw an image of Daniel Hood holding his pistol close to Tidwell's forehead and pulling the trigger. Jesse fired his pistol one more time.

After the last shot the only sounds left in the little canyon were Heidi's muddled sobbing and Jesse's labored breathing. Jesse's shoulders sagged as the nervous rush of energy of the battle left him. He still clutched the smoking pistol in one hand while both arms hung limply at his sides.

All at once he remembered the warrior that he had struck with his rifle butt. Expecting to be attacked from behind he whirled around. There was no sign of life from either of the warriors at the fire ring. Jesse breathed a sigh of relief. Gasping for air and feeling weak in the legs he put his pistol away and moved slowly toward Heidi.

Heidi was sitting up. Jesse spoke softly to her, "Heidi, everything is all right now. Heidi, it is me, Jesse, I am your friend." With her head buried in her hands she continued crying.

Jesse picked up a blanket that was lying on the ground and put it over her bare shoulders. He tried again, "Heidi, I know your father and mother, Mr. and Mrs. Adolph Baumgartner."

The blank look in Heidi's eyes was replaced with one of recognition as she looked up at Jesse. She sniffled, and used the blanket to wipe her runny nose. Heidi then nodded her head that she understood.

Other than a few bruises on her arms and face and a few scratches Heidi didn't appear to be badly hurt. "If you can walk I want you to get up and I'll take you beyond this camp site."

They went past the bend in the trail where Heidi wouldn't be able to see the carnage that was behind her. "You sit down here, I'll find some water and we can wash up. After that I need to round up some horses. Don't you worry; you're all right now. Won't be any harm come to you."

Jesse found a clay jug full of fresh water and some rags. He washed the blood from his face and arms before going back to care for Heidi. He was relieved that she hadn't tried to leave.

"Heidi, can you wash yourself off while I round up some horses?"

She had been looking at the ground. Without saying anything Heidi reached out for the rags.

"Good girl, I am not going far. You clean up and sit tight."

Most of the Indian's horses were still inside of the main room where the four bodies were. The horses had been spooked by the shouting and shooting. They tried running away but several of them couldn't leave. They had gotten tangled up in the tether rope and their hobbles and remained inside of the big room.

Jesse found his own horse and then worked to free a sturdy looking mare from the tangled ropes. He tied the two horses to some scrub brush and decided to capture Spotted Horse's big stallion.

If people could see me on that stallion they would know that I killed Spotted Horse or stole it from him. There is one way to make sure that they will know that I killed him. I'll take his scalp and put it with the two scalps that Woman put in that little leather bag.

Other Indians will think twice about challenging me if they see these possessions that had belonged to the great Spotted Horse. Horrible as that seems it may be like getting a free pass through the rest of this hostile country.

He returned to Heidi with the big black and white stallion and another grisly trophy in his small saddle pouch.

He mounted the mare that he had caught and helped Heidi onto his horse. Then keeping a tight grip on the rope he led the nervous stallion along with the horse that Heidi was on out of the canyon.

The wind had come up and was blowing briskly causing dust to swirl around over the landscape. They ducked their heads against the wind and headed toward where the wagon train had stopped. Heidi's sniffling was heard over the sound of the blowing wind. Jesse tried his best to reassure her that they would be all right and would soon reach the wagons. Sometime later he realized that she had stopped crying. He turned in the saddle to look at Heidi.

With red rimmed eyes Heidi looked at Jesse and for a fleeting moment a weak smile played over her lips.

Later they had barely come into view of the wagon train when the entire group of settlers surged toward them on foot.

Heidi's mother was the first to see them. "Heidi, Heidi" She called out in a loud voice as she sprinted toward them. Mrs. Baumgartner's yelling managed to frighten the black stallion. He reared and tried to pull away from Jesse. The stallion almost succeeded in pulling Jesse off of his horse. Thankfully Mrs. Baumgartner realized that her actions were causing the stallion's tantrum. She put her hand over her mouth and came forward at a slower pace. She was the first to reach Heidi.

One of the settlers came forward and took the stallion's lead rope from Jesse. The others crowded around the two young people and everyone started asking questions and giving thanks to the Lord and congratulations to Jesse for performing the "miracle rescue."

At the same time a band of twelve Indians were nearing the little blind canyon where Jesse had rescued Heidi. The leader was a stately distinguished looking man who was at least six foot and six inches tall. His well-muscled arms and his legs were so long that his feet almost touched the ground while he sat astride his pony. This man not only had a magnificent strong body but he was also very handsome. He looked and carried himself like royalty.

One of the braves spoke, "The wind is blowing hard, yet there are some buzzards circling over that little blind canyon."

"Big Bear look." He pointed, "I see two ponies dragging their halter ropes as they graze. Something is wrong down there."

155

Big Bear sent one of the braves into the canyon. "See what is there and come back and tell me what you find."

The scout returned and reported to Big Bear. "There are four horses running loose and six dead men. Two were killed with arrows and the others were shot."

"Only one of the dead was scalped."

Big Bear acted annoyed that he didn't have more information. "Why would only one be scalped? Three of you go back and look for sign. Maybe that will tell us more."

When the three returned one came forth to report to Big Bear. "The wind has ruined many of the tracks, all but the newest ones. There were three horses that left the canyon together. They were all Indian ponies. I believe two were being led. One of those being led left big hoof prints."

It angered the big leader that he didn't have more information about what happened in the little canyon. He, Big Bear, an Arapaho Chief had come far to see the famous warrior called Spotted Horse. He felt like there was not a warrior from any tribe that was a match for Big Bear. He wanted to meet this famous Spotted Horse, who had killed many warriors, counted many coup and had stolen many horses. Big Bear wanted to measure himself against such a warrior.

With an angry jerk of the reins he kicked his horse into a gallop and headed down onto the canyon floor. He growled to himself, *Fools, I will see for myself.*

At the entrance of the big room Big Bear slowed his pony to a walk. With a keen eye for observation he recognized how each man had been killed and where they lay.

When he saw a big body lying face down he dismounted to have a closure look. This is the only brave that had lost his hair. The corpse in front of him was naked below the waist.

Big Bear was very curious, why take one man's hair and not the others. He rolled the corpse over on his back. When he saw the scarred face and torso Big Bear was shocked. He jumped back in surprise. "This is Spotted Horse!!!!"

He looked closure, "Come here," he called out to the others. "This is the great warrior I came to see. He did not die easily. See he was shot four times before he died."

One of the braves spoke, "They must have had a white women as a captive. That is why he is naked."

Big Bear called out, "Come, there is still enough light to track the horse with the big hooves. I must meet a warrior that has such great medicine that he could kill Spotted Horse."

The wind had continued blowing making the shifting dust an annoyance to Big Bear and his band as they approached the wagon train. Big Bear signaled to the others to stop. They were well out of rifle range of the settler's wagons.

There was much nervous excitement among the people in the wagon train when they saw a dozen Indians within a short distance of the wagons. They called out to Jesse to come and take a look.

Jesse stood at the perimeter of the wagons and studied the band of Indians as their ponies milled about. "Someone get that stud horse for me. No need to saddle him, I'll ride him bare back. Henry I want you to bring me your rifle and tie a thin leather strap onto the barrel. Make sure the rifle is properly loaded."

While waiting for his horse and rifle Jesse stared at the dozen Indians milling about in the wind. He was trying to identify what tribe they belonged to. Finally one of them separated himself from the others and rode alone to within a short distance of the wagons.

Jesse could see that the Indian was a very tall well-built man. He was the tallest man that Jesse had ever seen. The tall Indian wore his hair in two braids; one on each side of his head. He had on a doe skin shirt. The front of the shirt was decorated with beads. His large moccasins were also decorated with beads. The Arapahos wore beaded clothes and had their hair braided.

He may be Arapaho. I hope that he is. There language is much like the Pawnee's language. Maybe I will be able to communicate with him using sign language and speaking the Pawnee tongue.

157

Henry brought his rifle to Jesse. Jesse went to where his saddle was lying on the ground and took something out of it and stuffed the object down in the front of his shirt.

When the other settler brought the stallion; Jesse sprang onto the stallion's bare back. With the rifle in one hand he decorated the barrel with what he had put under his shirt and rode out to meet the big Indian.

Stopping in front of the tall Indian Jesse greeted him in the Arapaho tongue, "Hebe". Than he waited patiently for the tall man to speak.

Surprised the tall Indian raised his eyebrows slightly as he did not expect to be spoken to in a familiar tongue. The tall man did not try to hide his dislike for the man in front of him. Holding his chin high in an arrogant manner he looked down his nose at Jesse. It was obvious that he thought very highly of himself and very little of the white man in front of him.

"You speak Arapaho?" He asks.

"Some, along with a little Pawnee and I can sign some." Jesse answered politely.

Big Bear thought that this slender young white man could not have killed six warriors and then rode away on the big animal. The tall man pointed at the black and white stallion. "That is Spotted Horse's pony. Why do you have his horse?" He demanded in an ugly tone.

Jesse took care to keep the barrel of the rifle pointing away from view of the arrogant Arapaho warrior. "Spotted Horse does not need this horse any longer so I took it and now it is mine."

From his superior height he looked down at Jesse. "I am Big Bear, an Arapaho chief." He had a sneer on his thin lips as he spoke.

Jesse looked directly into Big Bear's eyes. He repeated, "Chief Big Bear, I claim this stallion because Spotted Horse doesn't need it any longer." Jesse lifted the barrel of the rifle high over the front shoulders of his mount and pointed it up in the air. The trophy that was tied to the barrel swung freely in the wind. All could see that it was fresh and not old and dried out.

Jesse spoke with firm authority, "And I took this from Spotted Horse; he does not need this anymore either. It too is mine."

Big Bear was startled to realize that this white man was the one that killed Spotted Horse. His eyes opened wide in surprise and his sneer disappeared. "Who are you?" He demanded.

Jesse answered in an even tone. "My white friends call me Jesse." Big Bear seemed agitated that this white man would waste his time.

Jesse continued looking directly and unwavering into the eyes of Big Bear. "That is my white man's name but the Pawnee, the Sioux and other nations call me, The Wind Spirit Warrior."

Big Bear had heard of the great medicine of the wind warrior. He looked again at Spotted Horse's big stallion and at Spotted Horse's hair at the end of the white man's rifle. He then knew for sure that the warriors in the canyon had encountered this man's wrath.

Satisfied that he had found the warrior who was powerful enough to kill Spotted Horse Big Bear reined his horse around and rode back among his braves and led them away.

Back at the wagon train Jesse slipped wearily from the back of the black and white spotted horse. Relieved that the confrontation was over; emotionally and physically exhausted he slumped to a sitting position on the ground while many members of the wagon train crowded around him offering congratulations and thanks for protecting them from the Indians.

Adolph rushed in to protect Jesse. "Shoo, you're like a bunch of old hens. Go away and let this poor man rest. Can't you see that he is all done in. He is tuckered out from rescuing Heidi and chasing those other heathens off. Now go about your business."

Albert and Frieda, an old German couple that were rarely visible came to Jesse's rescue. "Let us take him to our vagon. Ve have a palate in the back of the vagon for him to rest on."

They helped Jesse into the rear of their wagon. He was asleep as soon as his head touched the goose down pillow that Frieda had supplied. Although he was exhausted he slept poorly. He tossed and turned and cried out when tormented with night mares of the events of

159

the past day. The bumping and jolting of the wagon as it navigated the ruts of the trail never woke Jesse from his troubled sleep.

It was noon the next day when Jesse suddenly sat bolt upright. He was looking out of the back tailgate of the old German couple's wagon. He was starring directly into the faces of two very large yoked oxen that were pulling the wagon behind them.

Frieda had been on the front seat with Albert. She heard Jesse stirring and knew that he was awake. She worked her way back to him and kneeled down behind him. She put her hand gently on his shoulder and spoke to him softly. "You are safe, everything is all right. I have food and water here in the vagon for you."

Jesse was content to spend the remainder of the day resting in the wagon. Sometimes he would sit on the lowered end gate with his legs hanging down swinging in rhythm with the rocking of the wagon. From the opening in the back of the wagon he was content to watch the fluffy white clouds roll gently along in the blue sky. The wagon rattled loudly along the trail causing two black and white magpies to take flight from the branches of some hackberry trees. The sights and sounds of nature brought a contented smile to Jesses face.

Evening came and the wagon train pulled to a halt. Henry came to where Jesse was still sitting on the end gate. "Rachel has fixed some potato soup and baked fresh bread this morning. We would like for you to join us for supper."

Jesse was pleased that Rachel had finally decided to forgive him for making her unload her books back in St. Joe. "I would be delighted to come and share a meal with you. I would like to wash the dust off of myself first."

During the evening meal Rachel still had the same superior firm attitude of command. That seemed to be her personality. However her attitude toward Jesse had softened considerably. She was not only cordial but down right pleasant toward Jesse during the dinner.

They had finished the meal and exchanged pleasantries. Jesse got up to leave when he turned to Rachel. "Rachel, I apologize for embarrassing you when I dumped your books. Even though it was the correct thing to do to rid your wagon of the extra weight I didn't have to try and make a fool of you. I hope that you will accept my apology."

For a brief second Rachel's features softened, however she didn't allow herself to smile. With her usual stiff necked manner she replied. "Mr. Brookes, I accept your apology."

With that brief exchange, they parted. Jesse made the rounds to check on the others in the camp. He found the stallion and his gelding and made sure that they were properly hobbled.

Alone with his thoughts he stood and gazed thoughtfully at the distant mountain peaks. A cloud formation was obscuring some of the peaks. The sun would disappear very quickly once it got behind the mountain peaks. It would be dark soon.

It won't be long before the wagon train arrives at Fort Laramie. That is where I had told Adolph that I would leave the wagon train. By now the trail from Laramie to Oregon is fairly well established. They won't have any trouble finding their way to their destination.

I doubt that they will probably need me anymore. They will get along fine without me. He scratched his head. *What am I to do with myself when we part company?*

I wonder where Spirit Woman is. Probably some brave has taken her as his wife.

I may go back to the Elkhorn River Country where her people have their winter camp and see if she is there.

The following days went by quickly and without incident. The wagon train reached the top of a small ridge. Below them the fort was visible in a bend in the Laramie River. The members of the wagon train whopped and hollered and threw their hats in the air as they celebrated reaching this major mile stone in their journey. They were one third of the way to their destination.

Recently the wagon train had passed many items that had been discarded from other wagon trains that had gone before them. The Baumgartner's wagon was moving passed a discarded piece of oak furniture when Mrs. Baumgartner called out to Jesse.

"Mr. Brookes, that is about the same piece of heavy furniture that you made Adolph unload from our wagon."

Jesse teased her, "If you want to stop; I'll help you load this one onto your wagon."

Mrs. Baumgartner laughed as she shook her head and waved good naturedly at Jesse.

They were now close enough to the fort that Jesse could see the Indian teepees outside of the fort. He shaded his eyes with his hand in an effort to identify what tribe that the teepees belonged to.

The wagon train came to a halt at the confluence of the Laramie River and the North Platte. The Laramie was at a normal level and appeared peaceful. It presented a beautiful picture with the slow moving current passing through willow covered banks. Occasionally red winged black birds would take flight from stands of cat tails bordering the river.

Jesse halted the wagon train about one half mile away from the Indian camp. Once he had seen that they were settled down he rode forward to the outskirts of the teepees in hopes of finding out what tribe was camped there.

As he neared the teepees he had an unfamiliar uneasiness in his chest. For some unexplained reason he was nervous. Just then he saw a male figure step from behind a nearby tepee.

He recognized the brave, it was Kuuruk. Jesse quickly dismounted and addressed him in a friendly tone. He was surprised at Kuuruks cool response. Jesse's first thought was to ask where Spirit Woman was.

Before he could ask that question Kuuruk quietly pointed to two figures walking on a hill in the not too far distance. One appeared to be a woman and the other a toddler child.

Soberly Kuuruk asks, "Is that who you are looking for?"

Excited, Jesse hurriedly mounted his horse and kicked it into a trot and headed toward the two figures. Before he got too close he dismounted and leading his horse he walked slowly forward to greet Spirit Woman. He was not sure how he would be received, it had been several months and she was walking with a small boy.

She stopped when she recognized Jesse, the boy sat down in the grass to play with some loose rocks.

Jesse had stopped several steps from Spirit Woman. He stammered, "Is that yours?"

Spirit Woman held her hands up with the palms up, shrugged her shoulders and answered with a smile. "No, silly man, it has not been that long since you have seen me."

"I am sorry to ask such a silly question. I was surprised, but I am happy to see you. Do you have a husband?"

Spirit Woman said nothing but she shook her head no. "And you?" She asks.

Jesse replied in a like manner by shaking his head no. He reached down and picked the little boy up. The little boy was delighted when Jesse put him in the horse's saddle. Jesse and Spirit Woman continued walking toward the Indian's camp. They walked slowly side by side.

"I am a scout for this wagon train. They are going on to Oregon. The trail is clearly marked so they could get along without me; except they are such an innocent bunch. They are good people but not smart about this country and its people. It would be best for them if I were with them."

"Woman, I have been thinking of you." He stopped and faced her. "Would you go with me to Oregon? No, what I really want to say is I want you to go with me."

Spirit Woman was silent. She reached for his rough hand and held it in both of hers; then she held his hand up to her face and kissed his fingers. Her eyes were moist with tears.

THE END

About the Author

Jackie Joe(Jack) Fetty was born in southwest Iowa.
He was the youngest of six children. Jack is a retired
doctor of optometry and lives with his wife of 54 years in the
Des Moines, Iowa area. Jack's writings include "Muddy Creek," and
"Rings of Gold."

Made in the USA
Charleston, SC
15 December 2016